There were no easy answers,

Meredith thought to herself.

Should she stay, respect Cooper's guidelines and keep her opinions to herself? Or should she run from her attraction to Cooper and the opportunity to get to know him and his daughter, Holly, better?

Distracted, Meredith thought about staying...and about leaving...until she heard a soft rap on her door. Holly peeked in. "I can't sleep," the eight-year-old said. "Can I sleep with you?"

Meredith patted the sheet. "C'mon."

Smiling, Holly hurried to the bed and jumped in. "Mommy let me sleep with her."

"You miss her, don't you?" Meredith asked, never forgetting how she'd felt after her mother died, how she still missed her. Holly nodded, and sidled a little closer to her.

Her heart was telling her to stay. It was a powerful message she couldn't ignore. For maybe the first time in her life, Meredith was going to listen...no matter what the risk. Because Holly needed her here, and maybe Cooper did, too.

Dear Reader,

Compelling, emotionally charged stories featuring honorable heroes, strong heroines and the deeply rooted conflicts they must overcome to arrive at a happily-ever-after are what make a Silhouette Romance novel come alive. Look no further than this month's offerings for stories to sweep you away....

In *Johnny's Pregnant Bride,* the engaging continuation of Carolyn Zane's THE BRUBAKER BRIDES, an about-to-be-married cattle rancher honorably claims another woman— and another man's baby—as his own. This month's VIRGIN BRIDES title by Martha Shields shows that when *The Princess and the Cowboy* agree to a marriage of convenience, neither suspects the other's real identity...or how difficult *not* falling in love will be! In *Truly, Madly, Deeply,* Elizabeth August delivers a powerful transformation tale, in which a vulnerable woman finds her inner strength and outward beauty through the love of a tough-yet-tender single dad and his passel of kids.

And Then He Kissed Me by Teresa Southwick shows the romantic aftermath of a surprising kiss between best friends who'd been determined to stay that way. A runaway bride at a crossroads finds that *Weddings Do Come True* when the right man comes along in this uplifting novel by Cara Colter. And rounding out the month is Karen Rose Smith with a charming story whose title says it all: *Wishes, Waltzes and a Storybook Wedding.*

Enjoy this month's titles—and keep coming back to Romance, a series guaranteed to touch *every* woman's heart.

Mary-Theresa Hussey

Mary-Theresa Hussey
Senior Editor

Please address questions and book requests to:
Silhouette Reader Service
U.S.: 3010 Walden Ave., P.O. Box 1325, Buffalo, NY 14269
Canadian: P.O. Box 609, Fort Erie, Ont. L2A 5X3

WISHES, WALTZES AND A STORYBOOK WEDDING

Karen Rose Smith

Silhouette

R O M A N C E™

Published by Silhouette Books

America's Publisher of Contemporary Romance

For my Aunt Rose Marie.
With love.

SILHOUETTE BOOKS

ISBN 0-373-19407-2

WISHES, WALTZES AND A STORYBOOK WEDDING

Copyright © 1999 by Karen Rose Smith

Books by Karen Rose Smith

Silhouette Romance

*Adam's Vow #1075
*Always Daddy #1102
*Shane's Bride #1128
†Cowboy at the Wedding #1171
†Most Eligible Dad #1174
†A Groom and a Promise #1181
The Dad Who Saved Christmas #1267
‡Wealth, Power and a Proper Wife #1320
‡ Love, Honor and a Pregnant Bride #1326
‡Promises, Pumpkins and Prince Charming #1332
The Night Before Baby #1348
‡Wishes, Waltzes and a Storybook Wedding #1407

Silhouette Special Edition

Abigail and Mistletoe #930
The Sheriff's Proposal #1074

*Darling Daddies
†The Best Men
‡ Do You Take This Stranger?

Previously published under the pseudonym Kari Sutherland

Silhouette Romance

Heartfire, Homefire #973

Silhouette Special Edition

Wish on the Moon #741

KAREN ROSE SMITH

lives in Pennsylvania with her husband of twenty-seven years. She believes in happily-ever-afters and enjoys writing about them. A former teacher, she now writes romances full-time. She likes to hear from readers, and they can write to her at: P.O. Box 1545, Hanover, PA 17331.

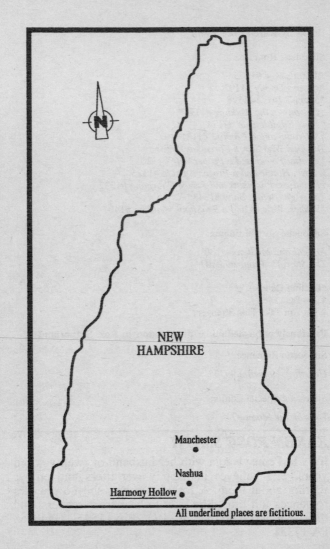

NEW
HAMPSHIRE

Manchester

Nashua

Harmony Hollow

All underlined places are fictitious.

Prologue

The stack of dirty dishes that threatened to topple over onto the counter reminded Cooper Murphy that his day wasn't nearly finished. He rubbed the back of his neck, wondering if the tension would ever leave.

"Daddy! Daddy! I'm ready for bed."

Cooper crossed the kitchen and hall in a few strides and called up the stairs. "Did you brush your teeth?"

Peeking around the corner of the stairwell, his eight-year-old daughter shook her head. "I forgot."

"Brush your teeth and pick out a book. I have a phone call to make. Then I'll be up."

"Okay," she agreed as her brown ponytail flopped over her shoulder and she limped down the hall.

Holly's limp broke Cooper's heart, and he couldn't keep at bay the swell of anger at his ex-wife. The accident had been her fault, but it was his that he'd let his daughter spend so much time with Tina in New York. Now that he knew what was going on, now that he was certain Holly didn't mean as much to Tina as her new life-style, Holly would be staying in Harmony Hollow with *him*. Permanently.

Back in the kitchen he snatched a letter from under a magnet on the refrigerator. He and Holly had managed just fine for the past two years. But that was before the automobile accident. He still remembered that night vividly—the hysterical phone call from Tina that they'd been in an accident, that Holly had suffered internal injuries along with a compound fracture below her knee, his frantic flight to New York. By the time he'd gotten there, they'd removed his daughter's spleen and set her leg and she was in recovery…

Taking a full breath, he came back to the present and thought about Holly's physical therapy appointments, all the schoolwork she'd missed, the back orders for his handcrafted furniture, and his best sales clerk out on maternity leave for two months. He hated to admit it, but he needed help. This was his busiest season, and he had to be at the store full-time. Although he'd depended on his elderly neighbor to watch Holly the past few weeks, he couldn't impose on her any longer.

He'd read Meredith Preston's letter of introduction. It didn't tell him much, just that she'd gone back to school and earned her teaching credentials. He'd called the references she'd given him at the college in Pennsylvania where she'd completed her coursework. Both of her teachers had recommended her highly. But most of all, he trusted Luke Hobart, his friend in Connecticut, who had suggested Meredith in the first place. She was Luke's sister-in-law. Luke had told him Meredith had returned to school after a divorce and was excellent with kids.

Cooper dialed the number on the letter.

"Hello?"

"Could I speak to Meredith Preston?"

"This is she."

He grinned at the proper English. A teacher all right. She might even wear her hair in a bun! Luke had said she was his wife's *older* sister, and her teachers had spoken about her maturity being an asset. "It's Cooper Murphy. Are you still interested in the teaching-housekeeping position?"

"Yes, I am."

"Your references checked out. But I wondered why you're willing to uproot your life to move to New Hampshire for a few months." There was a pause, but he waited. If she wasn't honest enough to answer the question, he wouldn't hire her.

"I've just become a teacher, Mr. Murphy, and I'm eager to start," she replied. "I've applied for several positions, but the school districts in this area are swamped with graduates. The idea of tutoring an eight-year-old for the summer appeals to me."

That sounded honest enough. "You *do* know you'll be living in my house to care for Holly. Do you have any qualms about that?"

"Just as you've checked *my* references, I've checked yours. I trust Luke's judgment. He and Becca assure me you're a man of honor."

"Becca has only known me for two years," Cooper murmured, embarrassed by his friends' compliment.

"But Luke has known you much longer. Are you trying to convince me *not* to take the job?" There was a hint of amusement in her tone.

He laughed, glad she had a sense of humor. "No. When can you start?"

"When do you need me?"

His gaze switched to the stack of dishes, the overflowing laundry basket he'd dropped at the laundry room door, and the grocery list hanging on the refrigerator. "Tomorrow," he answered wryly.

"I'm not sure I can manage that...."

"I was kidding."

"I can leave tomorrow and be there on Thursday. Will that work?"

Meredith Preston sounded intelligent, capable and decisive. He would bet she wore wire-rimmed glasses with her bun. "Thursday will be fine." As he gave her directions to the farm, he could feel the tension in his neck start to ease.

Help was on its way.

Chapter One

The pitch-black night reminded Meredith she had more determination than sense as she turned down a gravel drive, hoping she hadn't made a wrong turn. She'd told Cooper Murphy she'd arrive tomorrow. Leaving Pennsylvania early in the morning, she hadn't intended to drive straight through. But as she'd covered mile after mile, she'd decided she wanted to start her new life today.

Maybe she was just scared. All of her life, when she'd been afraid, she'd charged straight ahead. Oh, she wasn't afraid of teaching and caring for an eight-year-old. She loved children. But she had no domestic skills. Raised in wealth, she'd never had to cook or clean. And on the day she'd married, her ex-husband had told her he didn't want mundane concerns taking up her time. Since charity work had always been important to her, Brian had encouraged her to put her energy into that until they had children.

But they'd never had children, and after her second miscarriage...

As she told herself once again to leave the past in the

past, she concentrated on the floodlights before her that illuminated a double garage. Praying she had followed the directions correctly, liking what she could see of a spacious farmhouse connected to the garage by a breezeway, she parked, stepped into the cool, early-June night and followed a brick path to the front door. She rang the bell and waited.

In the distance an owl hooted, startling her. She rang the bell again.

The porch light went on and the door opened. Meredith smiled at the little girl who answered in a calf-length nightgown printed with colorful teddy bears.

"Hello. I'm Meredith Preston. Is your dad around?"

The child must have recognized her name because she said, "You're my teacher!"

"I hope so."

"Dad says I'm not supposed to talk to strangers, but if you're going to live with us, you're not a stranger. He's in his workshop. I'll show you."

Meredith's smile widened as the eight-year-old motioned her to follow. "Are you sure you shouldn't just go get your dad?"

"I'm sure."

Meredith followed the little girl, instantly aware of Holly Murphy's limp. Luke had told her that Cooper's daughter had been injured in an accident and missed three months of school, but her brother-in-law hadn't gone into detail, implying Cooper would probably want to fill her in himself.

They crossed a short hall into a country kitchen. The large white gas range was instantly intimidating. Meredith had lived on salads, yogurt and deli takeout during the years since her divorce. Her condo's beautiful kitchen hadn't seen much use. At least she was familiar with a microwave and dishwasher. Here the appliances, the knotty pine cupboards and long, off-white counter begged a cook to try out new recipes. When she'd stopped for lunch, she'd found a bookstore and had bought three cookbooks to get her started.

Holly headed for the back door. "Out here."

A light burned outside a two-room workshop about fifty feet from the house. Meredith kept step with Holly, who chattered all the way to the workshop. "He's way backed up because of taking care of me."

"He is, is he?" Holly's words showed a maturity not many eight-year-olds possessed.

"Yep, but he says it's okay cause I'm more important than his special orders." Holly opened the door, and they both stepped inside.

Wearing safety goggles, Cooper Murphy stood at a long workbench.

"Hey, Dad!" Holly called above the buzz of the sander.

When he looked up and saw them, he slid the goggles to the crown of his head where they ruffled his thick brown hair. His eyes were an even darker brown. He was at least six feet two with broad shoulders, and the way his denim shirt and worn jeans fit, she could tell his build was muscled and hard. The lines around his eyes and the angle of his jaw added to his rugged appearance.

Switching off the sander, he came forward, away from the machine.

"I arrived a little early," Meredith explained with a breathlessness that was totally unlike her. To make up for it, she extended her hand. "I'm Meredith Preston."

Taking her hand in his very large one, he gripped it, then quickly released it. But the imprint of the heat and roughness of his clasp remained.

"I thought you'd be older," he said in a deep voice that seemed as wary as his eyes were guarded.

She squared her shoulders. "I'm thirty-one."

His gaze passed over her shoulder-length blond hair, her blue-striped knit top and white jeans. It was an appraising male look that made her wonder if she passed muster. Then she was annoyed with herself. The failure of her marriage and Brian's infidelity had led her to become much too self-critical. She'd gone back to school to prove she could have meaning in her life that had nothing to do with her wealth or attracting a man.

Yet awareness of herself as a woman seemed all encompassing with Cooper Murphy standing a few feet away, male power emanating from him as if it was some exotic cologne that could make her need as a woman again.

"Luke said you were Becca's older sister."

"Two years older. And we're actually stepsisters." Now why had she added that? She and Becca had become as close as birth sisters since Becca had met and married Luke Hobart.

Holly tugged on Meredith's elbow. "Do you know how to ride?"

"Holly…" Cooper warned.

"Dad won't let me ride Gypsy since my accident."

Meredith stooped down to Holly's eye level. "Is that how you were hurt?"

Shaking her head, Holly answered, "Uh-uh. It was in a car in New York with Mommy."

Cooper crossed to Holly and scooped her up into his arms as if she were four instead of eight. "You, young lady, belong in bed."

His daughter wrapped her arms around his neck. "Carry me to the steps?"

"Sure will. Then I'll get Miss Preston's luggage."

"Meredith," she said to both of them.

Holly grinned at her and asked in a pretend whisper, "*Can* you ride?"

With a conspiratorial wink and a smile, she whispered back, "Yes, I can."

Cooper just frowned and carried his daughter to the house.

As Holly waved and ascended the stairs, Meredith followed Cooper out to her car. She was glad she'd traded in her BMW for this less ostentatious sedan when she'd started back to school, deciding to leave pretensions of wealth behind her.

When she opened the back door of the car, Cooper lifted out a large suitcase, while she gathered a stack of books and a duffel bag that held a few puppets and learning tools.

"I can come back for them after I take this in," Cooper offered.

"I'm fine," she said, liking his sense of chivalry but determined to prove she didn't need it. She didn't know why he'd expected her to be older, but she was going to convince him older wasn't better.

When he carried her suitcase upstairs, she followed, admiring the beautiful grain in the banister rather than the snug fit of Cooper Murphy's worn jeans. He took her to the room farthest down the hall and pushed the door open. A star-patterned country quilt covered the pine cannonball bed. The pine dresser and nightstand looked aged.

"I've seen the furniture you made for Luke and Becca for their dining room and guest bedroom. It's beautiful. Did you make this, too?"

He laid her suitcase on the bed. "No. My grandfather did. He taught me everything I know."

The fondness in Cooper's voice drew her gaze to him. "You spent a lot of time with him?"

"I came here to live when I was sixteen and never left."

Avoiding Cooper's gaze as well as her attraction to him and a curiosity to know more about him, she dropped her duffel bag on the bed by the suitcase and set the books on the small writing desk.

"Are you hungry?" Cooper asked.

Her stomach growled at the thought of food. "I don't want to put you to any trouble."

"No trouble. There's pizza in the refrigerator we can warm up in the microwave."

When their eyes met, Meredith's throat went dry. Cooper's dark regard seemed to try to see much more than her blond hair and her green eyes.

"You drove straight through?" he asked.

"You said you needed me as soon as possible, and..." She paused.

"And?" He was looking even deeper.

"And no one's needed me in a very long time."

Silence pulsed between them along with something much more elemental. Finally he arched a brow and asked, "Are you always this honest?"

"I try to be," she murmured, not liking the vulnerability she was feeling under his gaze.

Whether he approved or disapproved she couldn't tell as he turned and left the room with the expectation that she'd follow. She wondered what other expectations he might have. For some absurd reason, she didn't want to disappoint him.

She'd disappointed Brian and he'd found someone else. *Get over it, Meredith. You do not need any man's approval.*

Hoping the thought would become a self-fulfilling prophecy, she followed Cooper to the kitchen.

Meredith Preston's footsteps were light behind Cooper as he crossed the kitchen. At least once a week he picked up a pizza for supper. It was his daughter's favorite food. But as he pulled the leftovers from the refrigerator, his mind wasn't on food but on another appetite he'd denied since his divorce. Meredith Preston awakened it with a vengeance. That silky blond hair, those sparkling green eyes, not to mention all the right curves...

Damn. He should send her packing in the morning. Yes, Holly needed a teacher. But not one who made him feel as if he'd been sucker punched every time she looked at him.

And he'd thought she'd wear wire-rims and a bun! Not in *this* lifetime. Why hadn't he asked Luke for details? Why hadn't Luke told him Meredith Preston looked more like a model than a housekeeper?

He'd find another teacher. He'd put an ad in the paper—

"Your house is lovely," Meredith said from somewhere over his shoulder.

Even her voice slipped over his nerve endings like a satin glove, arousing in its softness. Geez.

"It was my grandfather's," he said tersely. Sometimes he felt as if he'd inherited too much, yet he knew he'd worked as hard as his grandfather to keep it, as well as to carry tradition into the next century.

He transferred the wedge of pizza to the microwave and set the timer. "So you're from Lancaster?" He remembered the address on her letter.

When she nodded, her hair brushed along her cheek

and he itched to finger it. What was it about this woman? What was wrong with him?

Needing to move away from her and a light scent that was so different from the heavy perfume Tina had worn, he took glasses from the cupboard and set them on the table. "Soda or cranberry juice?"

"Cranberry."

He should have guessed she'd go all natural. Everything about her was.

The microwave beeped, and they reached for the handle at the same time. His fingers tangled with hers, and the softness of her skin aroused him. She pulled away as quickly as he did, but not until their gazes collided, held, and he saw golden sparks of awareness in her green, green eyes. Green like a mysterious forest...

The phone rang, startling them both.

Cooper took a deep breath and snatched the receiver from the wall. "Murphy here."

"Cooper, it's me."

He couldn't keep his voice from going cold. "Hello, Tina."

"How's she doing?"

"She's still limping. She still gets up in the middle of the night, afraid to go back to sleep because she doesn't want to have bad dreams."

"She called and left a message on my machine this afternoon."

"You're her mother. Of course she wants to talk to you."

Meredith lightly tapped his arm. When he looked up, she pointed to the living room and moved away. He realized she was not only beautiful, but perceptive, too.

"But you try to prevent her from calling me, don't you?" Tina asked, pulling him back to their conversation.

He ran his hand over his face and held on to his temper. "I'd like to, but I don't because she loves you. I don't understand why. You neglected her long before you left, putting that damn book before her—"

"I *never* neglected Holly. I only wrote when she was in school, after she was in bed. *You're* the one who couldn't accept me having an interest outside of you and Holly, and making jelly or baking bread."

Everything about Tina set him on edge these days. They hadn't fought when they were married. He'd been determined to have a different type of marriage from his parents'. But since their divorce, he and Tina rarely agreed. Maybe he *had* resented the time she'd given to her writing because he'd felt her moving emotionally farther and farther away. "You proved what was important to you when your agent sold the movie rights to your book and you moved to New York. You wrote about glitz and glamour and that's what you wanted. Fine. But Holly doesn't go anywhere near your champagne-and-caviar life-style again."

"It's *not* my fault my driver skidded on the highway—"

"It's *your* fault Holly was curled up in the back seat without a seat belt, way beyond her bedtime, because you dragged her along to a party where she didn't belong!"

"I can't talk to you when you're being unreasonable. Tell Holly I'll call her soon."

The sharp click of disconnection echoed in Cooper's ear. Tina never did know how to stand her ground, to hang in when the going got rough. They might have worked out their problems if she'd given him half a chance, but she hadn't wanted a marriage...or the responsibilities of motherhood. She'd wanted the brass ring and she'd grabbed it for all she was worth.

Now he had to make sure Holly recuperated fully, that she would always stay safe. It was his duty and it was his vow. He'd made it as he'd sat by his daughter's bed after the accident, after her surgery, when he didn't know if she'd ever come home again.

Hanging up the phone, he remembered the pizza and Meredith Preston waiting in the living room.

There was no place in his life for an attractive teacher who would be more of a distraction than he wanted to handle. He was asking for trouble if he let her stay. Yet he couldn't turn her out tonight. She was probably tired and hungry and deserved a good night's sleep.

He strode to the living room, then stopped in the doorway to watch Meredith as she examined the books in the alcove beside the fireplace. When she turned to face him, there was concern in her gaze, as if she knew his conversation had been exasperating. Maybe she'd overheard some of it.

"The pizza's yours. I've lost my appetite. I'm going out to the shop," he added, knowing he was being abrupt but figuring that was best for both of them. "The white towels in the bathroom are fresh. I'll see you in the morning."

Before he got lost in her green eyes, he headed for his workshop and the peace he always found there.

The dull buzz of woodworking equipment urged Meredith to peer through the window over the sink as she rinsed her dish. She hadn't heard much of Cooper's phone conversation, but she *had* heard his deep voice rise as he'd talked to his ex-wife. Did he blame his ex-wife for Holly's accident? Had it been her fault?

Not that it was any of Meredith's business.

Opening the dishwasher, she found it full of clean

dishes. She was tired but too wired to sleep. If she emptied it, she'd officially begin her job as housekeeper. She *could* do this. Cooking couldn't be all that difficult if she followed the directions in the cookbooks she'd bought. But she suddenly wished she'd paid attention to Becca's skill in the kitchen whenever she'd visited her.

Ten minutes later, with the dishwasher emptied, she took one last glance at the light shining from the windows in the workshop, then went upstairs. A long shower relaxed her, and as she brushed her hair, a wide yawn proved she was ready for bed. As she sat on the edge of the bed and reached for the light, she thought she heard a noise in the hall. It wasn't loud enough to be Cooper. There was a brush and a shuffle. Meredith opened her door.

Holly was sitting on the top step, leaning against the wall, a stuffed horse in her arms. When Meredith stepped into the hall, the eight-year-old scurried to her feet. "I...uh...I thought you were sleeping."

Tying her belt on her cotton robe, Meredith approached her. "I was just about to crawl into bed. It's getting pretty late."

"I know," Holly murmured.

"Can't you sleep?"

The eight-year-old shook her head.

"Were you waiting for your dad to come up?"

She nodded and hugged her horse tighter.

Meredith held out her hand to Holly. "Why don't you hop in bed and I'll tell you a story?"

"Do you know one about a horse?" the eight-year-old asked hopefully.

Obviously horses were Holly's favorite animal. "I'm sure I can think of one about a horse."

The pink-and-white bedspread in Holly's room matched

the frilly curtains at the windows. But the pictures of horses taken from magazines and taped to the closet doors—as well as the riding derby and crop hanging on a clothes horse—told Meredith that Cooper's daughter liked horseback riding better than playing with dolls.

Meredith pulled a cotton-candy-colored chintz chair over to Holly's bed. When Holly scampered under the sheet and looked up at her expectantly, she began.

As she wove together a tale of a little girl, her horse and an adventure into the enchanted forest, Holly's eyes grew heavy. She soon lay on her side on her pillow, listening, struggling against sleep. Finally her eyelids stayed closed and her breathing became even. Meredith reached for the lamp on the nightstand.

But as she turned the switch, Holly asked, "Will you stay here till Dad comes up?"

Meredith's own eyes were heavy-lidded but she couldn't deny the little girl's request. She wondered if Holly waited up for Cooper every night. "I'll stay. You close your eyes and dream about riding Gypsy."

When Holly smiled at her and reached for her hand, Meredith's throat tightened, and she knew she'd made the right decision coming to New Hampshire.

It was almost midnight when Cooper climbed the stairs. After he reached the upstairs hall, he saw the open door to the guest room, a lamp still shining inside. As he passed Holly's door, the hall light spilled into the shadows and he spied the bedroom chair pulled up to the bed. Pushing open the door, he found Meredith asleep, her hand being held by his daughter.

As he crossed the room, the tableau made his breath catch. His voice was gruff when he bent to Meredith. "What are you doing in here?"

Her eyes flew open, and as she straightened her cheek was very close to his lips. He could smell her shampoo and the faint, underlying scent of her perfume. Yet if she'd just taken a shower, it must be soap...

Hell, what did it matter?

"Did Holly have another nightmare?" he asked tersely.

Fully awake now, Meredith shook her head slowly, her gaze falling on his lips. Then she sat up straight, drawing away from him. Leaning close to his daughter, she murmured to her, "Your dad's here now. I'm going to my room."

Holly opened her eyes, saw him there and smiled. "G'night, Daddy." Then she turned on her other side and went back to sleep.

Meredith stood and went to the door; he followed her to her room. "What was *that* all about?" he asked, trying to pull his attention away from how her robe draped over her breasts. It was a soft, green material, its V-neckline trimmed in lace.

"After my shower, I heard something in the hall. It was Holly, settling on the top step to wait for you," Meredith explained.

His body was responding to the sight and scent of her, in spite of his resolve to remain unaffected. "What do you mean she was waiting?"

When Meredith tightened her belt, he was even more aware of the slimness of her waist. She met his gaze directly. "Is Holly ever asleep when you come up?"

"Of course, she is. I put her to bed about eight-thirty, and I don't come up till eleven or so. Why?"

"She was waiting on that step as if she's done it many times before."

"You're wrong."

"Or maybe you just want me to be wrong. What kind of accident did she have?"

"It was an automobile accident that never should have happened." The bad weather, a combination of ice and rain, had plagued the East Coast all day. Tina should have stayed at home and had their daughter in bed that night, not at a party for adults who didn't give a whit about Holly. But then, Tina hadn't been willing to make necessary sacrifices to be a good mother. That's why she'd left. Traveling, book signings and rubbing elbows with celebrities had held an allure for her she couldn't resist.

"Does she have bad dreams about the accident?" Meredith pressed.

"Now and then."

"She might be afraid to go to sleep until she knows you're up here."

"Look, Miss Preston, just because you've had some training as a teacher doesn't make you an expert on my daughter!"

"It's Meredith. And I'm not claiming to be an expert. But I remember when my mother died and all the fears I had that I'd lose my father and sister, too. Every night I'd go to my sister's room or she'd come to mine. I couldn't sleep until she was there beside me, and even then I was still afraid."

He remembered his own childhood, his parents fighting, how scared he was alone in his room. He was surprised Meredith would share something so personal with him. If she was truly trying to help his daughter, she needed to know the score.

"Holly *knows* I'm here for her. She knows I'll never leave like Tina did, and I'll never let anything bad happen to her again."

"You can't promise that. No one can."

The truth in Meredith Preston's conclusion hit too close to home. He hadn't been able to prevent Tina from leaving. And when Holly was with her mother, he was powerless to protect her. But that's why Holly wouldn't be going to New York again. Still, he didn't like a stranger making him face a reality he'd rather ignore.

"I'll be here for Holly and protect her till my dying breath," he vowed in a low voice, vehement in his determination.

Meredith stood before him, not defensively or intent on making a point, but with concern in her eyes. Her lips were so sweetly curved, her skin porcelain delicate. And even though she'd stirred up turmoil he kept in a tight-lidded box for Holly's sake, he realized the urge to kiss her was much stronger than the urge to send her packing.

"Holly is very lucky to have you as a father," his new housekeeper said softly.

He didn't know what to say to that, so he didn't say anything.

After a few moments of silence she asked, "What does Holly like for breakfast?"

He cleared his throat. "Cereal. I usually just grab a cup of coffee."

As if she'd put some thought into her first day with Holly, Meredith said, "Tomorrow I'd like to just become familiar with your daughter's routine and look through her schoolbooks with her. I want her to become comfortable with having me around."

Shouldn't he tell this pretty teacher not to unpack her suitcase? Shouldn't he tell her he was going to look for someone older—without silky blond hair, without a kissable dimple in her cheek when she smiled?

Damn! What was he getting himself into?

He remembered the sight of Holly's hand in hers. "We'll talk about it in the morning," he decided.

Meredith looked puzzled at his brusqueness, then she took a step back into her room. "All right. In the morning."

With a nod, he turned away from her and a temptation he didn't need or want. When Tina left, he'd decided he was finished with women. He wasn't going to change his mind because of sparkling green eyes that saw entirely too much.

Chapter Two

After Cooper tended to the horses and dressed for work the next morning, he resolved the issue of Meredith Preston. She seemed to have his daughter's best interests at heart. He'd give her a week, see how Holly responded to her, see how well she took care of the chores that had kept him from turning out special orders, let alone staying on top of the quarterly bookkeeping.

So he was attracted to her.

All he had to do was remember his marriage to Tina and their divorce, and his hormones would settle down. He was too old to let lust run his life or rule over good sense. Picking up the phone in his bedroom, he called his neighbor to tell her, at least for the time being, Holly had a nanny.

The aroma of brewed coffee wafted up the steps as he opened his bedroom door after the call. When he checked Holly's room and found her still asleep, he went downstairs, satisfied with his decision, glad he didn't have to worry about what he and Holly would have for supper.

Entering the kitchen, he stopped when he spotted Meredith sitting at the table, mug of coffee in hand, her head bowed over a book. She glanced over her shoulder when she heard him and smiled.

That smile practically turned his resolve to keep his distance from her into a desire to get to know her much better. Reminding himself he needed a housekeeper, not a bed partner, he nodded and walked over to the coffeepot.

"Sure you don't want breakfast?" she asked. "I can make toast, scrambled eggs—"

"No, thanks." He quickly poured himself a cup of coffee then gestured to the refrigerator. "The number for the store, Holly's doctor, and other emergency numbers are on that green sheet."

She pushed her chair back and rose. When she reached the refrigerator, she took the paper and examined it. Stepping close to him, she asked, "Is that a seven or a four?"

Damn, if he couldn't still smell her shampoo. His gut tightened. "It's a four." So much for a cup of coffee. After a sip that practically scalded his lips, he set the mug on the counter. "I've got to get going." Before he took another whiff of her, before she could smile at him again, he went to the doorway leading to the laundry room and breezeway.

"Mr. Murphy?"

With a sigh, he turned. "It's Cooper."

"What time would you like supper?"

"Unless I get tied up, I should be home by six. Make sure Holly rests this afternoon. I'll see you tonight."

He thought he heard her call a "goodbye" and "have a good day," but he didn't linger to find out.

The morning passed quickly as Meredith went through Holly's schoolbooks with her to find out how far she'd fallen behind. She hoped to speak to Holly's teacher but wanted to talk to Cooper about it first. *If* he ever stayed in the same room long enough to have a conversation. There was a tension between them that was as exciting as it was exasperating. She hadn't come here for more than a job that could add meaning to her life. But when Cooper looked at her...

She realized she'd missed a man's appreciative regard as much as his intimate touch. She'd liked being married, being a partner rather than standing alone. Except too late she'd discovered Brian only wanted a perfect partner. His infidelity and the possibility that she might never be a mother had made her feel more insecure than she'd ever felt in her life.

Fear of being hurt again, of not being woman enough for a man, had kept her from dating since her divorce, though Becca's union with Luke had given her renewed hope that some marriages were made in heaven. Still, she remembered the pain of betrayal all too well and wasn't sure she could risk giving her heart or trusting a man ever again.

Holly pointed to the chapter heading in her science book. "This is the last one I read before I went to New York with Mom. Are we going to eat lunch soon? I'm hungry."

The meat keeper in the refrigerator held sliced ham and cheese. Meredith could handle making sandwiches and peeling carrots for Holly's lunch. Preparing supper was another matter. She'd found a recipe that looked easy, but she needed to go to the grocery store for a few ingredients.

"We can have lunch right now. Afterward I'd like to drive into town for groceries."

"Oh, can we? That'd be great. Except..."

"What, honey?"

"Daddy doesn't let me ride with anyone else. He drives me everywhere. I don't know if he'd be mad."

"I'll call him and ask."

Meredith took the green sheet of paper from the refrigerator and dialed Murphy's Furniture. The woman who answered put Meredith on hold until a few moments later when Cooper picked up. "What's wrong?"

"Everything's fine. But I'd like to come into town this afternoon to pick up a few things for supper, and Holly thought you might object to her riding with me. If you want me to take care of her, you'll have to trust me."

Silence met her words and she wondered if she'd approached the subject too bluntly. But Cooper seemed like the type of man who would prefer honesty over tact.

"Put Holly on."

Meredith gave the phone to the eight-year-old. "He wants to talk to you."

Cooper must have asked Holly if she wanted to go.

"Uh-huh. I can tell her what I like. What you like. I promise I'll put on my seat belt." Holly looked up at Meredith and smiled. "Okay. And I'll rest when we get back." She handed the phone to Meredith again.

"She obviously wants to go with you," he said. "And I know it's only a few miles but—"

"I'll be careful, Cooper. I promise."

There was a pause until finally he added, "Buy what you need. In my room there's an envelope on the chest. Use the money in there. I'll see you tonight."

When Meredith hung up the phone and looked over at Holly, she smiled. Cooper Murphy had grudgingly put his daughter's safety in her hands. She felt honored and a bit frightened, wondering if this was a little of what it felt like to be a parent.

The afternoon sped by as quickly as the morning. When

Holly went upstairs to rest, Meredith set out all the ingredients she needed to make beef Stroganoff over rice. After Holly came downstairs following her nap, she watched out the window as Cooper's daughter took a carrot to her horse in the paddock and spent a long time talking to her.

Although Meredith had planned her time and followed directions in the cookbook to the letter, dinner wasn't quite ready when Cooper pulled into the driveway. The flour in which she'd dipped the meat had puffed all over the counter. The rice had boiled over but still wasn't cooked, and although she'd checked the meat often, it wasn't getting tender. She added the sour cream anyway just as she smelled something offensive. It didn't take her long to figure out the peas had burned. She'd started them too high and forgotten to turn them down.

Cooper stepped into the chaos, his nose wrinkling as he caught the smell.

Squaring her shoulders, Meredith acted as if supper was exactly as it should be. "Everything's almost ready," she said cheerfully. "I'll call Holly if you want to wash up."

His gaze swept over the kitchen, the messy stove and counter, the perfectly set table with a bouquet of flowers at its center, then it lingered on Meredith. She knew her cheeks were flushed from standing at the stove, and flour streaked her jeans from where she'd wiped her hands.

"Where *is* Holly?" he asked as his eyes seemed to dally on her face until she wondered if she'd streaked her cheek with flour, too.

"With Gypsy. She promised me she wouldn't go inside the paddock."

"I almost called to check if you were back okay this afternoon."

"But you didn't."

"As you said, I have to learn to trust you. But I don't trust easily, Meredith."

The message was clear—she'd have to earn his trust. "I understand."

He came closer to the stove. "Do you?"

She nodded. "I'm divorced, too. I understand disappointment and dreams that will never become more. It changed the way I look at the world."

"And men?" he asked in a low voice.

"Especially men," she admitted, gazing into dark brown eyes.

"Did you want the divorce?"

"When I—yes, I did." She couldn't go into the details. Not with a stranger...and not when she felt as if something had been lacking in her.

"I didn't," he countered. "At least not then. Now I realize Tina and I should never have married. Holly is paying for our mistakes."

"But you wouldn't *have* Holly if you hadn't married."

The lines around his mouth eased and a smile curved his lips. "I shouldn't need someone to remind me." He cocked his head pensively. "I bet you're the type of person who counts her blessings every night?"

"I don't have one as precious as Holly to count."

The lid on the pot with the beef Stroganoff popped up and down. Meredith snatched it off, and as she stirred the thickened sauce, she realized the meat had stuck to the pan.

Cooper's deep voice slid over her shoulder. "I'll change and be back in five minutes."

Meredith rolled her eyes and sighed. Five minutes...before she served the first dinner she'd ever made.

* * *

Dinner was terrible, and why Holly or Cooper didn't mention it, Meredith didn't know. The meat was tough, the rice overcooked, the peas tasted burned, even though she'd only used the good ones from the top. Thank heavens she'd tossed a salad and bought dinner rolls. The pièce de résistance was the Jell-O that hadn't quite gelled. She'd thought briefly about trying to whip up a chocolate mousse...

Her cavalier attitude about cooking had to go. She needed some expert help before tomorrow night!

Cooper tried to spoon the gelatin into his mouth and finally pushed it away. "Holly, do you want to help me tend to the horses?"

His daughter shook her head. "I'll help Meredith clean up."

His brows arched in disbelief. "You'd rather clear the table than groom Gypsy?"

"I'll be down after I help."

Following Cooper's glance to the stove and countertops, Meredith knew he was thinking cleanup could take a while. But he didn't comment on the debris, just playfully tugged on Holly's ponytail and went outside.

Meredith picked up Holly's plate as well as her own and took them to the sink.

"You don't know how to cook, do you?" Holly asked.

Meredith thought about making up some excuse about a strange stove and learning the settings.

"I won't tell Dad if you convince him to let me ride Gypsy again."

Cooper's little angel with the trusting brown eyes knew how to use a situation to her benefit. "I won't agree to blackmail, Holly. If you want to tell your dad I can't cook, you go ahead. By tomorrow night if I can't figure out how to make a decent meal, I'll tell him myself."

"You will?"

Meredith nodded.

"What if he gets mad?"

"I'll deal with it."

"Mommy doesn't like to make him mad."

To Meredith that meant that Cooper's ex-wife avoided confrontation whenever she could. "Sometimes the only way to solve problems is to talk them out…whether someone gets angry or not."

Holly seemed to think about what she'd said. "Now I guess you won't want to ask Dad if I can ride Gypsy."

Meredith set the plates in the sink and clasped Holly's shoulder. "I want what's best for you. I'll talk to your dad when I think the time is right. Okay?"

"Soon?" Holly asked hopefully.

Meredith smiled. "Soon."

"Do you really think you can learn to cook by tomorrow night?"

"With a little help." Meredith winked and rinsed the dishes.

Cooper supervised Holly, lifting her so she could reach Gypsy's hindquarters with the grooming brush. She'd come rushing into the barn, saying Meredith didn't need her help cleaning up after all.

Supper had been…interesting. But he guessed Meredith wasn't used to a gas stove. Hopefully meals would improve as she learned more about it.

Setting his daughter on the ground, he took the brush from her. When he heard light footsteps, he looked up and saw Meredith coming through the barn door. Everything about her seemed bright and pure and sparkling. As she came closer, the smell of hay and damp earth and horses faded into the expectation of something sweeter, something almost intoxicating.

"It's almost eight-thirty. Would you like me to help Holly get ready for bed?"

They hadn't outlined Meredith's specific duties. The idea of hiring a housekeeper was much easier than the circumstances of having one. All day the memory of Meredith sitting in the dark, holding his daughter's hand had played in his head, and he knew he couldn't ignore Holly waiting up for him last night.

Crouching down in front of his daughter, he said, "Meredith thinks you don't fall asleep at night until I come upstairs. Is that true?"

Holly shuffled hay on the ground with her sneaker, then she glanced over his shoulder at Meredith. "Sometimes," she murmured.

"Most of the time?" he asked.

She looked down at her sneakers again, but nodded.

Taking his daughter's chin in his hand, he waited until her gaze met his. "Can you tell me why?"

Her eyes glistened. "I'm afraid I'll have a bad dream and you won't be there."

He gave her a huge hug, trying to tell her he'd *always* be there.

As Meredith came closer, she offered, "Holly, I can stay upstairs and read until your dad comes up. Do you think you can fall asleep knowing I'm there?"

Cooper released Holly and stood. "I can't ask you to—"

"You hired me to take care of Holly. And I love to read. So why don't we try it for a few nights and see what happens?"

"What do you think, small stuff?"

Holly smiled and nodded.

"Go on up to the house. We'll be there in a few minutes," he added.

"You don't have to come, Dad. Meredith can tell me a story. She's good at it."

A twinge of regret pinched him. He looked forward to the bedtime ritual of reading his daughter a story. "I'll still come up and tuck you in."

After Holly patted Gypsy one last time, she left the barn.

"She's taken to you," he said quietly, surprised it had happened so fast.

"I've taken to her. On the calendar I noticed she has an appointment for physical therapy tomorrow morning. Do you want me to drive her?"

This is what he'd wanted, wasn't it? Someone to help so he could catch up in his business and his life? "I don't know why it's so hard for me to let you do the job I hired you for," he muttered.

"Maybe because you have to let go of Holly a little bit for me to *do* my job."

Because of the pull toward Meredith, he reminded himself why he was so protective of Holly. "I don't trust Holly with anyone but me. I used to trust her mother, but that was a mistake I won't make again."

"Do you share custody?"

Even reminding himself of Tina's abandonment couldn't keep his attention away from Meredith's lips. "Her mother has liberal visitation rights, but from now on that visiting will take place here."

Gypsy nuzzled Meredith's shoulder, and Meredith rubbed the horse's neck. "Does Holly talk about the accident?"

"Only when she has bad dreams."

"Do you mind if I talk to her about it?"

"Not if it will help her sleep better."

"I'd like to call her teacher, too."

Cooper could tell Meredith was efficient and thorough, and that gave him more confidence in her ability to care for Holly. "Feel free. She'll only be in town until next week. She visits her sister in Canada every summer."

"Is there a reason Holly didn't try to keep up with schoolwork?"

When he picked up the grooming brush Holly had left on the top rung of the stall, he answered, "The accident was serious, Meredith. Too serious to think about schoolwork while she was in New York the first month. When I brought her home, I just wanted her to spend time in the sun and get healthy again. So I didn't push it."

"You've both been through a rough time." Meredith's voice was soft with understanding, as if she knew he'd almost lost his daughter.

He needed her to understand. And he realized he needed...

Meredith's blond hair was golden under the glow of the barn's light, and her eyes were as green as midsummer's most verdant leaves. She was as close as his arm's reach and as he had since last night, he wondered how she'd taste...how she'd respond to desire. His desire.

As he bent toward her, Gypsy whinnied softly. Coming to his senses, he straightened and took a step back. He didn't need a kiss with Holly's nanny complicating his life. And he had a gut feeling it would definitely complicate his life.

Meredith's cheeks flushed. "I'd better go help Holly." Turning, she headed for the door.

"Meredith?"

She stopped and looked over her shoulder.

"I'd appreciate it if you'd take Holly to physical therapy tomorrow."

"I'd be glad to," she murmured and left the barn, leaving him with the feeling that he'd backed away in the nick of time.

Because one kiss with Meredith Preston would never be enough.

Cooper's footfalls sounded on the steps, and Meredith held her breath. In the barn earlier… She was sure Cooper had been going to kiss her. She'd been so curious, so excited about the possibility that she hadn't been thinking about the consequences. Apparently he had.

What was wrong with her, anyway? Brian had taught her the pain of infidelity. Her miscarriage had indelibly engraved scars of loss on her heart. Why would she even want to contemplate kissing a man again, let alone more? Her desire to get closer to Cooper confused her. Since her divorce, she'd been perfectly happy with her life *without* a man in it. Why this sudden penchant for a kiss from Cooper Murphy tonight?

She heard him stop at Holly's room. Then once again his boots on the hall floor made her heart beat faster. When he rapped on her door, she let out a breath, rose from the rocker at the window and crossed the room to open the door.

Cooper's beard shadow was dark and sexy. His camel-colored workshirt with the rolled-up sleeves contrasted with his tanned forearms and dark hair. He was strong and solid with an honesty that attracted her as much as his broad shoulders and rugged features.

"Did Holly fall asleep after I went outside again?" he asked.

"I checked on her twice and she was sound asleep."

His brown gaze passed slowly over Meredith's face and paused on her lips. "I...uh...packed her bag for physical therapy tomorrow. She needs her bathing suit for the pool. I put the address with the bag."

"We'll be fine, Cooper. Do you want me to call you when we get home?"

"No. As you said, I'll have to learn to trust you...with Holly."

The air between them filled with the same electricity she'd felt from the moment she'd arrived.

His eyes sparked with golden desire as he said in a husky voice, "I almost kissed you in the barn."

"I know," she murmured.

"I thought the feeling would go away."

"But it hasn't?" she asked, her voice a bit breathless.

He shook his head. "It definitely hasn't." Slowly, as if he was giving her the chance to back away, he bent his head. When she stayed perfectly still, he brushed his lips over hers for a few moments. It was an erotic sensation— one that had her yearning for more.

But before the kiss could become full-blown, he raised his head. "Good night, Meredith. I'll see you in the morning."

As he turned away, she put her hand on the doorjamb for support. He went into his room and shut the door.

He was a stranger and she longed to feel his arms around her. It made absolutely no sense.

Hoping she could sort out her feelings, remembering Brian's betrayal, reminding herself of her miscarriages and how her husband had reacted to them, she closed her door and slipped into bed. But when she turned off her light, she could still see Cooper's face.

While Holly went to the paddock to say good-morning to Gypsy the next day, Meredith called Becca at the Evergreen Foundation where she now worked with Luke, who was CEO.

Meredith and her younger sister, Paula, had always believed Becca's mother married their father for his wealth. Consequently, they'd kept their stepmother, as well as Becca, at a distance. It was only after Luke Hobart entered Becca's life that Meredith had really come to know her. Now she felt as if they were sisters.

"Hi, Meredith," Becca greeted her. "What's up? Is everything okay with Gran?"

Becca and her son had left Pennsylvania to start a new life with Luke over two years ago. But they'd lived with her grandmother for many years after Becca left home and still worried about her as well as missed her.

"Gran's fine," Meredith reassured her. "Paula's taking good care of her." Paula had moved in with Gran soon after the two women had decided to become partners. They'd bought Becca's restaurant when she married Luke and moved to Connecticut.

"Becca, I'm calling because I need help. I'm in New Hampshire at Cooper Murphy's. He hired me! But I tried to cook supper last night and it was a disaster." She told her stepsister exactly what had happened.

"So you want me to tell you how to cook a decent supper in twenty-five words or less?" Becca asked with some amusement.

"No, just tell me where I can learn fast."

Becca laughed. "All right. Find out if Harmony Hollow has a friendly butcher. He can tell you all about cuts of meat and how long to cook them. And keep the meals simple. Most men like meat and potatoes." Then she gave Meredith some easy ideas for side dishes.

"You're a lifesaver."

"True," she laughed. "How do you like Cooper and Holly?"

"Holly's a wonderful child. I'm going to love teaching her. And Cooper..."

Something in her voice must have alerted Becca because her stepsister asked, "Remember the advice you gave me once about being careful?"

"Yes."

"That goes double with Cooper, Meredith. Tina hurt him badly, and he hasn't let a woman get close since."

She remembered how close he had been last night...the brush of his lips. "And I haven't let a man get close since Brian. But Cooper...isn't anything like Brian."

"Uh-oh. Is my warning too late?"

"No! I just— Never mind. I'm here to teach Holly and that's what I'm going to do, though my dad thinks I'm crazy. I called and left a message where he could reach me. His service must have paged him because he called back before I left and gave me the third degree. He simply doesn't understand why I can't be satisfied hostessing bridge clubs!"

"And all the explaining in the world won't change his mind," Becca suggested. "You know that as well as I do."

"I know. Maybe someday we'll spend more than a few rushed minutes together and really get to know each other." Accepting what she knew she couldn't change, she said, "Give my love to Luke and Todd. If I can't find a friendly butcher, I'll call you again for explicit instructions."

"On how to cook?" Becca teased.

"What else?"

Becca laughed again. "Good luck. I'm here if you need me."

Meredith was glad she and Becca had finally bridged the stepsister gap.

Checking the clock on the wall, Meredith realized she had to corral Holly or they'd be late for her appointment. As she went outside and took a deep breath of New England air, heard the swish of the maple leaves in the breeze and felt the sun on her face, she knew she'd made the right decision coming here.

She was definitely ready for a new life.

When Cooper set foot in the kitchen Friday evening, only good smells met him. Meredith was arranging slices of roast beef on a platter. But before he could take a second whiff, Holly came rushing into the room and gave him a hug.

He grinned down at her. "Hi. How was PT today?"

"I worked *really* hard. And Meredith asked Miss Nancy if I can ride Gypsy. She said I can!"

He held Holly by the shoulders. "Whoa, there. Miss Nancy doesn't make that decision. I do." His gaze locked on Meredith's. "And you had no right asking or trying to interfere."

"I wasn't interfering. Holly has mentioned wanting to ride several times and—"

"No. She's not getting on Gypsy. Not yet."

"Dad…" Holly pleaded.

"No. That leg isn't strong enough to ride a bike, let alone control a horse."

"I told you he'd get mad," Holly mumbled to Meredith.

"I'm not angry, Holly," Cooper said to his daughter. "At least not with you. Meredith should have talked to me first before raising your hopes. Now, it looks like supper's ready. Let's eat before it gets cold."

"I'm not hungry," Holly answered in a low voice. "I'm going up to my room."

All Cooper could think about was getting his daughter healthy and strong again. He pulled out her chair at the table. "Sit down, Holly. You're not going to mope about this."

For a moment Holly looked as if she might disobey him, but then she did as he'd ordered.

The meal was delicious, but silent, and Cooper didn't like the looks he was getting from Meredith, which were anything but apologetic. After Holly picked at her meat, baked potato and green beans, she asked, "Can I go upstairs now?"

Raking his hand through his hair, he replied, "Go ahead."

Holly left the table, her uneven steps sounding down the hall.

When his daughter was out of earshot, Meredith set down her fork. "Now I see why Holly's afraid to talk to you. You get angry or give orders. Just how long do you think that's going to work with her?"

The spots of color on Meredith's cheeks, as well as the judgment in her green eyes, made his voice as cold as steel. "And just how long do you think you'll keep your job here if you come between me and my daughter?"

Chapter Three

"Are you telling me you'll fire anyone who sees a problem with Holly and brings it to your attention?" Meredith asked, not intimidated by his tone or his stern expression.

"And exactly what problem is that?"

Knowing she was probably crossing a line, but concerned about Cooper as well as Holly, she answered, "You can't protect her from life, and if you keep her from doing what she loves, she'll resent it and eventually she'll defy you."

"So you're a psychologist now? Or maybe I didn't see the crystal ball you brought with you."

Ignoring his sarcasm, she reasoned with him. "I'm using my common sense, Cooper. Holly loves Gypsy, and she loves riding. If you keep her from both because of some fear of yours for her safety, she'll pull away."

He tossed his napkin on the table and stood. "Two weeks ago she still had a cast on her leg. She might have that limp for the rest of her life."

Meredith stood, too, to put herself on equal footing with him. Well, almost equal footing—she still had to look up. "Her physical therapist believes as she strengthens her leg, the limp will fade. Haven't you talked to her about it?"

His shoulders squared. "Of course I have. But I'm being realistic."

"No, what you're doing is preventing Holly from making a full recovery. If you limit her, she'll never know what she *can* do."

"If I don't limit her, she'll get hurt again," he returned firmly. "Now, if you can't abide by the rules I set down for my daughter, you'd better pack your suitcase and drive back to Pennsylvania."

If she couldn't really help Holly, what good was her presence here? Besides, this attraction to Cooper was better left unexplored. "Maybe I should. I'll think about it and give you my answer in the morning."

He looked surprised, as if he'd automatically expected her to back down. Then the gold sparks flared in his eyes, and anger edged his voice. "Fine. You do that. I'll be in my workshop if Holly wants to know where I am."

When he left the kitchen, he let the screen door slam behind him.

Meredith let out a breath and some of the tension that always gripped her when Cooper was nearby. Her gaze fell on the roast beef that, thanks to a friendly butcher, had tasted just as roast beef should. Her cooking had been a success but her championing of Holly had not. It had seemed so easy to her. Ask the expert. Get her facts straight. Then persuade Cooper.

But reason wasn't guiding him. His worry about Holly was making him rigid.

Should she stay, respect his guidelines and keep her opinions to herself?

Or should she run from her attraction to Cooper and the opportunity to get to know him and his daughter better?

As she cleaned up the kitchen, Meredith faced the facts squarely. If she stayed and got attached to Holly, leaving would be difficult at the end of the summer. But if she left now, she'd be guarding herself as she had since her divorce. If she kept her heart closed to prevent pain, wouldn't she prevent herself from feeling joy, too?

There were no easy answers.

After Meredith cleaned up the kitchen, she coaxed Holly out of her room to play a board game until bedtime. As he had the night before, Cooper tucked his daughter into bed then went back to his workshop, saying a polite good-night to Meredith. After a shower, she settled into bed to read...and to think.

She'd only turned a few pages when rain began to fall outside. Tree branches scraped against each other and the house as the wind picked up, whistling under the eaves and the clapboard.

Distracted, Meredith thought about staying...and about leaving...until she heard a soft rap on her door. Holly peeked in. "I can't sleep."

"Is the storm keeping you awake?"

The eight-year-old nodded. "Can I sleep with you?"

Meredith didn't know how Cooper would feel about it, but Holly looked lonely and scared and Meredith couldn't bear that. Folding back the covers, she patted the sheet. "C'mon."

Smiling, Holly hurried to the bed and jumped in. "Mommy lets me sleep with her."

"You miss her, don't you?" Meredith asked, never forgetting how she'd felt after her mother died, how she still missed her.

Nodding again, Holly sidled a little closer. "Daddy's mad at her 'cause she wants to write books. She doesn't want to live with us anymore."

Meredith understood divorce and some of the reasons for it. But she couldn't understand any mother leaving her child. If only she could have carried her babies...

She might not agree with Cooper's overprotective ways, but she understood the reasons for them. Her heart was telling her to stay. It was a powerful message she couldn't ignore. For maybe the first time in her life, she was going to listen...no matter what the risk. Because Holly needed her here, and maybe Cooper did, too.

Rain still splattered against the windows as Cooper climbed the stairs around one, satisfied he'd made headway on a dining room set that was a special order. When he stopped at Holly's room and saw her bed was empty, he panicked for a moment. But then sense prevailed as he strode toward Meredith's open door.

Light spilled across Meredith's blond hair as she lay facing his daughter, a novel propped open atop her hip. He guessed they'd been talking and had fallen asleep. Had Holly been afraid of the storm? There had been rain and ice the night of her accident.

Had she talked to Meredith about Gypsy? Or more important, about thoughts and maybe fears she wouldn't share with him? *Was* his desire to protect Holly limiting her?

Meredith had given him something to think about, though he'd gotten angry when she'd challenged him. Since his divorce, anger simmered close to the surface—except when he worked out back.

Quietly rounding the bed, he slid his arm under his daughter's shoulders. Ready to lift her into his arms, he paused when she opened her eyes.

"I'm going to carry you back to your room," he murmured.

"Can't I sleep with Meredith?"

Suddenly he was gazing into Meredith's green eyes, shadowed with vestiges of sleep.

She propped on her elbow. "I don't mind."

With a sigh he knew he couldn't deny Holly this security she apparently needed. "All right." He straightened and adjusted Holly's covers, all too aware of Meredith's nightgown slipping over her shoulder, and the creamy skin above her breasts.

"Cooper?"

Meredith's voice stopped him, and he waited.

Her gaze tenderly settled on his daughter. "I want to stay."

Relief washed over him, and he told himself he didn't want to go through the hassle of finding someone else. "We'll talk about it in the morning."

Turning away from the bed, he went to the doorway. When Meredith switched off the light, he closed the door, realizing the image of her in her nightgown had burned an imprint in his mind. Hopefully sleep would erase it.

If it didn't, he'd find something that would.

Meredith was eating a bowl of cereal with Holly the next morning when Cooper came into the kitchen from outside and headed for the coffeepot. When the phone rang, he picked it up. After he listened for a few minutes, he turned to his daughter.

"It's Marsha's mother. Marsha's missed you and wants

to know if you'd like to go over there to play and stay for lunch.''

"Can I?"

Cooper was silent for a few moments, then nodded.

Holly jumped up from her chair and hugged him around the waist. "Thanks, Dad. I'll go get some stuff ready."

After he made arrangements with Marsha's mother, he hung up and brought his coffee mug to the table.

Meredith remembered Cooper coming into her bedroom last night, bending close when he'd murmured to Holly. She'd come awake with the instant awareness that the hour was late and he was near enough to touch. Early this morning she'd heard him go downstairs and leave the house to tend to the horses.

"Holly was frightened by the storm," she explained.

"It was windy and raining the night of the accident." His large hand gripped the mug a little tighter.

"Before she fell asleep last night, she talked about it. How it happened. The trip in the ambulance to the hospital."

"She must have been conscious in the ambulance. She never told me that," he said in a low voice.

After a strained silence, Meredith said, "I'd like to stay if you still want me to, but I have one condition."

His brows arched.

"Even if you don't agree with me on what I think is good for Holly, promise me you'll hear me out before you say no."

"I thought the employer set the conditions," he said in a wry tone.

With a small smile, she asked, "Isn't negotiating part of any employer-employee relationship?"

His probing brown gaze raked over her blue-plaid cotton blouse, coming to rest at the vee her collar made at her breasts. "You should have become a lawyer instead of a teacher."

"It's a small concession, Cooper. Unless you don't want me here. Unless you'd rather hire someone else." She couldn't help holding her breath as she waited for his answer.

His eyes narrowed, then his shoulders seemed to relax. "My daughter likes you, and I think she feels attached already or she wouldn't have come to you last night. She's had enough upset lately, and I don't want to add to it. As far as your condition goes, I'll listen. But just remember I have final say on anything that concerns Holly."

And what about anything that concerns the two of us?

The question had popped into Meredith's mind, and just as quickly she popped it out. There *was* nothing between the two of them but a brush of lips that barely qualified as a kiss. He'd made it clear that he'd like her to stay because of his daughter—not because of any sparks or electricity she might be imagining.

Politely and professionally she extended her hand. "I can agree to that."

When his fingers gripped her palm, when his gaze locked to hers, her thoughts were anything but professional and polite. Something about Cooper awakened everything womanly within her that had been asleep. It might be his height and strength or his rugged features, but she was more sure it had to do with his sheer being, the type of man he was. Solid. Strong. With unshakable values that wouldn't change with his needs. This man would believe in fidelity.

Yet she couldn't really know that.

Could she?

When he released her hand, the heat of his handshake remained.

"Are you going to the store today?" she asked.

He shook his head. "I try to take Saturdays to work out back."

"I need to go to the butcher shop. I can take Holly to her friend's house if you want to work."

Cooper took a swallow of coffee, then stared at her over the rim. "Are you pushing or just trying to make my life easier?" There was dry amusement in his tone.

"Maybe a little of both."

Standing, he took his mug to the sink. "You can take Holly to her friend's house, Meredith. But just realize if you keep pushing, I'll probably push back."

If his words were meant as a warning, she didn't take them that way. Instead, she looked on them as a challenge she looked forward to meeting.

After Meredith returned from delivering Holly to her friend and made a stop at the meat shop, she blessed Becca for her suggestion to make friends with a butcher. Wrapping the meat she wouldn't use until next week, she placed it in the freezer. She'd numbered each pack to match the numbers on her slips of paper. While the butcher had talked about the cuts of meat and the best method for cooking them, she'd taken detailed notes. Sliding her notes into her pocket, she headed for the laundry room and the cleaning supplies. She'd probably have enough time to dust downstairs before she fixed sandwiches for lunch.

She was dusting the bookshelves beside the fireplace when she heard a car door. Stepping to the window, she saw a small car speed away. A flutter of white under the cedar at the corner of the gravel lane caught her eye. She thought about ignoring it...

Leaving the front door open, she walked across the

brick path and down the driveway. Under the cedar, she saw a white shopping bag and hurried her pace. As she heard a mewling sound, she reached inside and found two kittens. Their eyes were open, but they couldn't be more than a few weeks old, too young to be separated from their mother. But at least they were both crying...at least they were still alive. She cuddled the two kittens in the crook of her arm and rushed through the house, to the kitchen.

Cooper was washing his hands at the kitchen sink. "I thought I'd get some lunch. You don't have to stop what you're doing on my account—" As he flicked off the spigot and turned, he saw what she'd found. "Kittens. What are you going to do?"

"Find a box. Keep them warm. Feed them. I need the number of your veterinarian."

He wiped his hands on a towel and came closer. "Meredith, they're really small, and they might not make it. Are you sure...?"

"They *will* make it. Don't even think they won't!" She felt tears come to her eyes.

He took her by the shoulders. "Whoa, there. What's going on?"

Ever since her miscarriages, she'd known how precious life was. She wanted to hold on to it, nurture it. But she didn't feel she knew Cooper well enough yet to explain. "We can save them, Cooper. I know we can."

After studying her carefully for a moment, he released her. "We'll do our best. Stay here with them. I'll be right back."

Meredith cuddled and cooed to the kittens, running her fingers over their downy fur until Cooper returned with a cardboard box, a soft towel and a pair of rubber gloves. After he carefully placed them in the box, the yellow tiger kitten nuzzled his thumb while the calico one meowed louder.

"How could anyone just dump them?" Meredith asked angrily as she continued to watch them.

Cooper took a box of straight pins from a drawer. "Maybe something happened to the mother."

"That's *no* excuse."

Holding the glove, he poked a hole at the tip of one of the fingers. "Warm up some milk. Thin it with a little water."

Meredith took a measuring cup and warmed some milk in the microwave, testing it with her finger at intervals. When it was just right, she handed the cup to Cooper and he poured it into the little finger of the glove. Then he tested the makeshift bottle by offering it to the kitten. Once the yellow kitten started licking and drinking, Cooper fixed up a second glove and Meredith coaxed the calico one into trying it. As both of them suckled, she looked up at Cooper. "They *are* going to be okay."

He was standing right at her shoulder, so close she could feel his body heat, smell a mixture of wood and male that sent her senses reeling.

"Why are they so important to you, Meredith?" His brown gaze wouldn't let her escape or turn away.

"Because I..." She'd kept the sadness inside, only letting it come to the surface in rare circumstances.

As if he knew she needed to be coaxed, as if he knew she wouldn't talk about it easily, he grazed her cheek with the back of his hand. "Meredith?"

Suddenly the words came pouring out. "I had two miscarriages. And there was nothing I could do. I tried to do everything right. Especially when I discovered I was pregnant the second time. But it just wasn't meant to be, I guess. I felt so helpless."

His gaze bathed her in understanding. "I'm sorry."

Tears welled up again, and although it had been over four years since her last miscarriage, she felt as if it had happened yesterday. "I thought I was over it."

"But you're not," he concluded gently.

She took a tremulous breath. "Deep down, I know that getting on with my life isn't the same as forgetting the loss. I'm not sure we can ever forget what we lose, though we pretend we can."

Cooper stroked his thumb over her cheekbone. His tender touch was as arousing as it was comforting. The golden sparks in his eyes told her he enjoyed touching her as much as she enjoyed being touched, and whether it was logical or not, she felt that she knew him very well.

Abruptly he stepped back and nodded for her to take the glove he was holding. "I think I have a hot-water bottle upstairs we can put in here with them. I'll be right back."

Whenever she and Cooper connected, he backed away. If she was smart, she would keep her distance, too. But the feelings that stirred where Cooper was concerned had nothing to do with being smart.

The yellow kitten stopped drinking and curled up against its sibling, its eyes closed. Meredith gently laid her finger over him and could feel him breathing. Soon the second kitten stopped eating, too, and both fell fast asleep.

The top shelf of the second floor's hall closet was stuffed with everything Cooper didn't use often. As he rooted for the hot-water bottle, he thought about Meredith and her miscarriages and the urge to kiss her that was becoming almost too strong to fight. That brush of lips against lips the other night had warned him to keep a lock

on his libido and his attention elsewhere. But Meredith's
maternal concern for those kittens, the glistening sadness
in her green eyes had almost drawn him into a situation
he knew he'd regret.

As if he didn't have *enough* regrets.

After he found the hot-water bottle, he snatched the
alarm clock far back on the shelf and grabbed two more
towels. Returning to the kitchen, he saw Meredith gently
petting the kittens, as if each stroke of her fingers could
instill in them the will to live. She obviously had better
maternal instincts than Tina. Any mother who could just
walk away from her child…

When Meredith looked up, she said, "They're so
small."

"But far enough along that we can help them," he
assured her, his resolution partly coming from the desire
not to let Meredith experience another loss. After he filled
the hot-water bottle, he wrapped it in a towel and placed
it near the kittens. They squiggled next to it, still seeking
comfort from each other, too. Then he wound and
wrapped the clock, placing it near them. "It's a poor substitute, but they might think it's their mama's heartbeat."

"Where should we keep them?" Meredith asked, her
voice husky. "I'll have to feed them every few hours and
keep the box clean. Maybe we can put them in my bedroom?"

"When Holly gets home, you'll probably get an argument from her. But that's fine." He was about to lift the
box, when Meredith rose from her chair and clasped his
forearm. "Thank you."

Her touch melted into him until he forgot the box and
the kittens and got lost in her green eyes. "No thanks
necessary," he said gruffly as he straightened and pulled
away, trying to break the spell. But she was standing be-

side him, feminine, fragrant and much too enticing to ignore.

"You're a good man, Cooper."

Then why had his wife left? Why did he feel as if he'd failed in being a husband, a provider, a man who could hold on to a woman for a lifetime? "You don't know me," he answered, with the bitterness of divorce still burning on his tongue.

"I know Luke says you're a good friend. I know you love Holly. I know I feel safe here."

"Maybe you shouldn't feel so safe," he growled as he studied her lips and anticipated pleasure.

"Cooper…"

"What do you want, Meredith? Do you want to satisfy your curiosity? Do you want to explore this tension between us? Do you want to get a little thrill so this summer won't be boring?"

He roughly took her chin in his hand. "Then let's get this over with so we can both forget about it!"

When he sealed his lips to hers, he expected to do it quickly, with a searing intensity that would scare her away. But he found the intensity caught him, and the seal held, and the heat urged him to wrap her in his arms and not let go.

Kissing Meredith was an explosion of thought and feeling and sensation that engulfed him before he had the chance to breathe. All he wanted was more of her. Urgently. Fast. He strained for thought and sense and couldn't find either.

Red-hot need jolted him as her breasts met his chest. When his tongue speared into her mouth, her lips parted without resisting. The taste of her made his body shudder with desire, with arousal, with an instinct that was too primal to deny. His mouth angled over hers, eager for depth and taste and texture. He felt her tremble as he invaded again and again with more need than finesse, more surprise than satisfaction. He couldn't remember ever wanting a woman like this with such vehement urgency. He'd married Tina because he'd wanted a family, because he'd thought love would grow, because he'd expected a marriage without the fights and bitterness he'd experienced as a child...

The thoughts seemed important but vanished as he stroked Meredith's silky hair, down her back. She was slender but strong, sweet yet fiery, too....

Suddenly her hands flattened against his chest and he felt the slight push.

The gesture registered, and he felt foolish and chagrined that he'd given in to base hormones.

Abruptly pulling away, he released her and raised his hands as if she was too hot to touch. "Curiosity satisfied?" he asked tersely.

"I never said it was curiosity," she murmured. "You did."

"Wasn't it the thrill you expected?"

"Cooper..."

He waved his hand to brush away polite words that she probably wouldn't mean. Before either of them got more embarrassed, he picked up the box. "I'll put this in your room. Don't worry about lunch. I'm going to keep working until I pick up Holly." Then he strode out of the kitchen, intent on getting on with his day...and putting Meredith Preston out of his head.

Cross-legged on the rug in her bedroom, Meredith watched Holly feed the yellow kitten. The eight-year-old had been excited and bubbling over with enthusiasm to care for the kittens when she and Cooper had returned home. They'd stopped on the way and bought a litter box and litter, two small bottles a child would use with a doll, along with rice cereal intended for babies. Cooper had gruffly explained it would give the kittens more nourishment when they could lap at it.

Then he'd disappeared into his workshop again.

Holly had rested minimally, eager to watch the kittens. Her chatter about her day with her friend made supper less strained. Cooper had taken two helpings of Meredith's meat loaf, but hadn't spoken directly to her. They would have to clear the air eventually, but she wasn't sure how. His kiss had been the most sensually stirring experience of her entire life. But how could she say that? How could she tell him…

"I'm gonna call Mommy and tell her about the kittens," Holly decided, scrambling to her feet. "But don't tell Dad, okay?"

"Why don't you want your dad to know?" Meredith was sure he'd see Holly's call on the phone bill.

"He gets grumpy when I talk to her."

"And you don't want to make him grumpy."

Holly shook her head.

"Go ahead and call. I'll run your bath water so you can get ready for bed when you're finished."

Holly's high voice, filled with excitement and laughter floated up the stairway as she talked on the living room phone. Apparently Holly had a good relationship with her mother despite Cooper's anger at his ex-wife. Meredith wondered if that anger was relegated to Holly's accident or if it had begun in the marriage.

After her bath, Holly sat in Meredith's room with the kittens in her lap. Stroking them pensively, finally she looked up at Meredith. "They don't have a mommy anymore. Think I could be their mommy?"

Meredith heard Cooper's footsteps on the stairs and her heart beat faster. "I think you can be their substitute mommy."

"Can I keep them in *my* room?"

Meredith glanced at Cooper, who stood in the doorway. "We'd better ask your dad."

"Please, Daddy, can I? I want to feed them and everything."

"Holly, you need your sleep," he decided in a firm tone.

"Daddy, please? I'll take a longer nap in the afternoon. Please?"

Meredith could see Cooper's demeanor soften as his daughter pleaded with him. He wasn't nearly as hard a man as he pretended to be.

Advancing into the room, he stopped by the corner of Meredith's bed. "You can keep them in your room. If you wake up when Meredith or I come in to feed them, you can help. But otherwise, we'll let you sleep."

"Oh, boy! I *know* I'll be awake."

Meredith saw Cooper's frown, and she suggested, "I think it's time to put you and the kittens to bed." Carefully she lifted the kittens from Holly's lap and settled them in the box.

When Cooper said he would read Holly a bedtime story, Meredith wished her charge good-night. Standing at her dresser, brushing her hair, she relived Cooper's kiss and lost track of time until she heard a knock on the door. She opened it, meeting Cooper's expressionless face and remote eyes.

"I'm going to spend tomorrow with Holly so you can take the day off," he said.

"All right. I can drive into Manchester or Nashua, maybe do some sight-seeing."

"And I'll feed the kittens around midnight before I turn in," he added.

"I'll set my alarm for three."

He looked relieved she wasn't arguing with him. "Don't worry about getting breakfast in the morning. Leave as early as you'd like."

It sounded as if he couldn't wait to get rid of her. As if... "Cooper, don't you think we should talk about this afternoon?"

Raking his hand through his hair, he frowned. "I think it's best if we just go on as if nothing happened. Don't you?"

Obviously the kiss hadn't affected him as it had affected her. Apparently it hadn't affected him at all except to make him wish he hadn't done it. Her divorce had taught her one thing above all others—to hold her chin high and keep her pride intact. "Fine. We'll just wipe our minds clear of this afternoon. I'll leave early tomorrow and come back late in the evening. Good night, Cooper. Enjoy your day with Holly."

And she closed the door in his face.

Holding her breath, she waited. But there was no repeat knock, no calling of her name. After a moment Cooper strode down the hall and descended the steps.

Wipe your mind clear, she thought.

Sure. It was as easy as making beef Stroganoff.

Chapter Four

Panic wouldn't do her any good.

Meredith's headlights had become more and more dim, finally blacking out completely on a deserted road in the middle of nowhere. It was strange. The engine ran, but she couldn't drive on these back roads without headlights.

She recalled a gas station about a mile back—a two-pump gas station that had looked deserted. But if she remembered correctly, there had been a phone booth. The problem was—even if she called road service, she doubted that anyone would fix her car on a Sunday night. She had to call Cooper to come and get her. She had no choice.

Driving at a crawl, she could barely see in front of her, with the last shades of gray dusk disappearing into black night. How would Cooper react when she called?

When she'd fed the kittens at 3:00 a.m., Holly had awakened and insisted on helping, though she'd hardly been able to keep her eyes open. Meredith had forgotten to set her alarm afterward and hadn't awakened until nine.

Checking Holly's room, she'd found Holly gone and the kittens fast asleep. Downstairs, Cooper had left a note, saying he'd taken Holly to church and that they'd fed the kittens before they'd left.

Realizing again Cooper preferred her absence to her presence today, she'd driven to Manchester, enjoyed a long brunch as she'd read the Sunday paper, then had begun to explore the area. In the early evening, she'd taken to driving the back roads around Nashua, enjoying the landscape that reminded her of home. She'd parked and hiked along a stream, discovered a covered bridge and immersed herself in the sights and smells of a June day in New Hampshire.

So different from the life she'd led a few years ago with its parties and tennis matches and shopping for designer dresses to impress her husband's colleagues. So different…and so very refreshing.

Until her headlights had dimmed and gone out.

Finally in the near distance she saw a light. The small office at the gas station was dark but the dimly lit phone booth welcomed her like an old friend. Quickly she dialed the road service number, giving her location the best she could under the circumstances. Then she hesitated before dialing Cooper.

Punching in the numbers, she waited. Cooper answered on the second ring, his deep hello reminding her of his kiss, his scent, his taste.

"It's Meredith. My headlights went out, and I'm stranded someplace outside of Nashua."

"How did they go out?"

"They just became dimmer and dimmer. The car runs fine, but I couldn't drive it on these back roads without headlights."

"You can't drive on *any* roads without headlights."

Ignoring his comment, she went on, "I called the road service number they gave me when I bought the car, but I'll need a ride back to your place."

"Where are you?" he asked.

That was the tough question. "I'm not sure."

"What do you mean you're not sure?" His impatience was obvious.

"I'm at a phone booth at a gas station that's closed. I'm not exactly sure where I am, but I can tell you how I got here." She could imagine him frowning in disapproval, so she launched into the directions she'd given when she called the 800 number. They included landmarks more than route numbers.

"You didn't use a map?"

"No, I was just exploring." The silence that met her made her feel like a foolish child.

"Give me the number on the phone in case I have trouble finding you." After he took the information, he added, "It should take me about half an hour. Don't make yourself known until you see the flashing lights of the tow truck or until you're sure it's me. When I see the light from the gas station, I'll beep the horn."

"Cooper, I'm sorry about this—"

"I'll be there as soon as I can." Without a goodbye, he hung up.

Meredith shivered in the cold, knowing she'd be a lot happier to see *him* than he would be to see her.

Exactly twenty-five minutes later, Meredith heard a vehicle in the distance and then the beep of the horn as it drew closer. Relieved, she climbed out of her car as Cooper's truck rolled to a stop.

The night had turned cold, and she hadn't brought a sweater, thinking she'd be back before she needed one.

Cooper met her at her car. "I'm going to check it out. Why don't you wait in the truck?"

With her teeth almost chattering, she followed his suggestion.

A few minutes later he climbed in beside her. "It might be the generator. Or the computer. Car workings these days are a lot more complicated than they used to be." He reached out to hand her her keys.

Their fingers touched...

"You're as cold as ice," he said tersely. Shrugging out of his jacket, he ordered, "Take this."

Leaning forward, she let him place it around her shoulders. His fingers caught in her hair and grazed her neck. This time the shiver that ran through her had nothing to do with the cold. His arm was a near-embrace as he tucked the jacket around her, and he was as close as a kiss. The faint scent of spicy aftershave teased her as the heat left in his jacket warmed her. It was wool... rough...his.

"Cooper, thank you."

Meredith's husky voice slipped past Cooper's defenses before he could move away from her. He'd had an enjoyable day with his daughter, but he'd found himself missing Meredith's presence. He'd told himself he was being ridiculous. She'd only stayed under his roof a few days. But as he'd cooked hamburgers on the grill, and dusk had settled in, he'd checked his watch every ten minutes.

When she'd called to ask for help, he'd heard the hesitation in her voice and had known she'd had no choice. Thinking about her on a deserted road in the dark had unsettled him more than he cared to admit. "I couldn't leave you stranded out here." He reached in front of her to draw his jacket around her. It was only fifty-five degrees, and she'd obviously gotten chilled.

"Where's Holly?" she asked, looking up at him.

"In bed, I hope. Our closest neighbor, Mrs. Macavee, came over to stay with her. She's helped me out a lot since Holly's accident."

The light from the phone booth spilled into the cab illuminating Meredith's profile, and he found himself asking, "Are you okay?"

"I'm fine…now."

The urge to protect Meredith, to keep her warm in his arms for longer than the moment, shook him more than the scent of her or the sweet curve of her lips.

"Cooper," she began, her voice hesitant.

"What?" he asked gently, thankful she was okay.

"Yesterday when you kissed me, I wasn't upset. I just needed time to think about whether I was making a mistake."

"Did you decide?" he asked, his voice husky.

She shook her head, never taking her gaze from his.

Maybe the kiss had been a mistake. Maybe a second one would be an even greater mistake. But not kissing her again seemed an absolute impossibility. The intimacy of the truck, the dark silence, the temptation to combine their body heat was too strong to resist. His lips inched closer to hers as he waited for her to lean back. She didn't, but stayed perfectly still. The world seemed far, far away…and Meredith was right here.

The kiss swept him into it, with a little less urgency than the last one…with a little more finesse. He aimed to give pleasure as well as take it. The cool air seemed to become a haze around them as his lips parted over hers. Her arm came around him, her fingers sliding from the collar of his shirt into his hair. It had been too long since a woman had touched him. Meredith was warmth and light and the passion he'd buried for the sake of responsibility.

Since she'd arrived, his dreams had been filled with erotic images that had aroused him in sleep. But she was so much sweeter than the image and much more arousing. Just her fingertips in his hair made him want them other places. His tongue stroked hers—tasting, exploring, searching for satisfaction. When she responded with a small moan, he slid his hand between them.

But when he pressed his palm along the curve of her breast, her breath hitched and she broke away. There was no doubt again that she wanted to stop.

"I guess you've made your decision." His voice was raspy with the need still thrumming through his body.

"I don't know if this is a mistake or not, Cooper," she replied in a shaky spurt of words. "It depends on what you want."

"I think it's obvious what I want. And pretty obvious you'd like to come along for the ride."

"Then kissing you *was* a mistake. I won't be used as…as some kind of release."

"That's what sex is," he growled, thinking about the lack of passion in his marriage, the depth of commitment he'd invested but Tina hadn't.

Meredith's response was low but firm. "I won't make love with a man again unless there's more involved than a few moments of pleasure." With that conclusion hanging in the cold air, she shifted closer to her door and stared straight ahead.

Make love.

He'd made love to Tina. He'd faithfully given her his desire, his body, his dreams. But it hadn't been enough. Making love left a man vulnerable. He would never put himself in a vulnerable position with a woman again.

When flashing yellow lights appeared on the road, he opened his door and climbed out of the truck to escape the sexual vibrations still humming in the cab, to let the cold air convince him he didn't need a woman—especially not one who saw sex as more than pleasure.

Kissing Cooper like that...practically asking him to kiss her again, had been a mistake with a capital *M*. The silence on the ride back to Harmony Hollow only emphasized the fact. He was a man with strong needs—the passion in his kisses proved that. Yet Meredith suspected the desire that had ignited between them hadn't been welcome, that he didn't understand it any more than she did, that he didn't believe it went deeper. How could he? How could *she?* She'd only known him four days.

She should be driving back to Pennsylvania, taking refuge in a life that had become calm and peaceful if not meaningful. Her father believed she was crazy for coming here. Was she?

Cooper drove around the compact car on the gravel drive and into the garage. Meredith opened the door, climbed out and headed for the door, needing time to sort her thoughts. But as she entered the kitchen, she found an older woman, her black hair streaked with gray, turning the page of a magazine on the kitchen table.

She gave Meredith a quick once-over and smiled. "I'm Alma Macavee. And I would guess you're the Meredith who Holly chattered about all during the church service this morning."

"She's the one," Cooper verified coming in behind her.

"Holly's in bed, but I don't think she's asleep," Alma told him, standing and closing her magazine. She walked toward the foyer.

"I'll walk you out," Cooper offered.

She waved him away. "Not necessary. If my arthritis weren't acting up, I'd have walked over instead of driven. Good to have met you, Meredith. If you need anything, just give me a call. My name's on Cooper's list."

"Nice to meet you, Mrs. Macavee."

The older woman glanced again at Cooper's jacket around Meredith's shoulders and smiled.

Cooper followed the older woman to the front door and waited until she was safely inside her car.

After Meredith shrugged off his jacket, she handed it to him. "Thank you."

As he took it he was careful not to touch her hand. "You're welcome."

Mrs. Macavee drove off and Cooper locked the door.

"Would you like me to check on Holly?" Meredith asked.

"There's no need. If she's awake, I'll let her know you're here."

They were back to employer-employee again. It was more comfortable and definitely safer than relating on a personal level. Holding the banister, she climbed the steps, suddenly very tired and very sad without being sure exactly why.

As she walked down the hall to her room, Cooper disappeared into Holly's. But a few moments later he called her name.

Tossing her purse onto her bed, she hurried to Holly's room. The eight-year-old was propped on pillows, the kittens sleeping in her lap.

Cooper was standing by the bedpost. "Holly wanted to say good-night."

Meredith approached the bed. "I didn't want to wake you if you were sleeping, but it looks as if you have company."

"I like having them in my room."

Moving to the other side of the bed, Cooper scooped up the kittens. "It's time for all of you to get some sleep."

Holly looked up at Meredith. "Are you okay?"

With a reassuring smile, Meredith sat beside Holly. "I'm fine." She gave the child a hug, knowing she had stayed awake to make sure no harm had come to her.

Cooper cleared his throat. "I'll get up around two to feed the kittens."

Meredith stroked Holly's hair then stood. "I'll set my alarm for six."

At the doorway she wished them both a good-night. Cooper's dark brown eyes were as remote as they'd been after their kiss. As Meredith stepped over the threshold, she heard Holly tell her dad, "Mommy called after you left. She wanted to talk to you, but I told her you had to go get Meredith."

Meredith didn't wait to hear Cooper's response, and a thought suddenly hit her right between the eyes. Maybe Cooper wasn't ready for more than sex with a woman because he was still in love with his ex-wife!

Almost a week later on Saturday afternoon, Holly swung on the wooden swing hanging from a centuries-old oak in the backyard. After vacuuming downstairs and starting laundry, Meredith glanced out the window at Cooper as he used the trimmers on a few overgrown bushes. The tension between them since Sunday evening had settled into a remote politeness. She'd wanted to approach him about an idea that would make science more interesting for his daughter, but he'd spent most of the morning in his workshop, and she'd hesitated to disturb him there. Now might be a good time.

He looked over at her as she crossed the yard toward

him. His discarded shirt hung over a fence post. The sweat on his shoulders gleamed in the sun, and as Meredith got closer, she wondered if this was a good idea after all. The brown hair on his chest curled in a T pattern that fascinated her as much as the snap on his jeans. They hugged his lean hips, dipping at his navel.

When she stopped before him, she forced her gaze to meet his. "I wanted to ask your permission to do some planting with Holly for her science lessons."

"What kind of planting?"

"A small garden with carrots, radishes and tomatoes. I'd like to take her to a nursery and show her the difference between annuals and perennials. Maybe plant a few of each. Teach her about earth worms and the soil."

He nodded. "That sounds like a good idea. I can run the rototiller in a patch to make it easier for you to plant. We used to have a garden. But Tina didn't like tending it, and I ran out of time."

Meredith had never actually tended a garden herself, but she'd watched Becca's flourish, and last week she'd read up on them in preparation for Holly's lesson. "Holly's enjoying watching the kittens grow. I'm hoping she'll learn by watching plants and vegetables, too."

"You're a good teacher, Meredith. I've looked over Holly's workbooks and papers. But I think I'll have a problem when she goes back to school in September. She believes you're more fun than sitting in a classroom."

Meredith laughed. "I have a lot more leeway. And it's only been a week. She might get bored with my methods of teaching, too."

"I don't think anyone would get bored with you." His voice went lower, and his eyes weren't as remote as they had been the past few days.

Her gaze dropped to his chest again and her heart raced.

There were beads of sweat in his chest hair that glistened in the sun. Her fingers itched to touch it...to touch him. She tried to will the sensation to go away.

"Meredith?" When his gaze caught hers, it was as if he'd read her thoughts, as if he shared the need to touch and taste and hold.

The ringing of the phone shattered the moment as well as the bond of anticipatory intimacy that always sprang up between them.

"I'd better get that," he murmured. "Tina and I have been playing phone tag all week."

As Cooper strode across the yard and laid the clippers on the edge of the concrete porch, he glanced back at Meredith. She'd gone to Holly and was pushing her on the swing. His daughter was growing attached to her. And Meredith's quiet confidence was giving Holly a renewed assurance that her world was stable. Last night she'd told Meredith that since the kittens were keeping her company, Meredith didn't have to sit upstairs and read after she went to bed. But Meredith had simply replied that she'd sit in the living room instead so she was only a call away if Holly needed her.

He couldn't figure out why Meredith was so damn distracting to him. The way she'd looked at him a few moments ago had made his blood hot...

As the phone continued to ring, he hurried inside and snatched it up.

"Cooper? It's Tina."

"I've been trying to return your call all week."

"I was in New Jersey doing book signings for my new release. I got your messages, though, but wanted to wait until we both had time to talk without interruptions. Are you busy now?"

"This is fine."

"How's Holly?"

"She's fine."

"Cooper..."

"What do you want to know?"

"She told me about the kittens."

He had to smile. "She's getting a kick out of them."

"She told me about Meredith Preston."

His radar went on alert. "I mentioned I was going to hire a teacher."

"I thought you meant a tutor. Not a live-in. How old is she?"

Tina had a right to information about Holly, but she was treading the line. "Meredith is thirty-one."

"And pretty?"

His fuse was getting shorter. When they were married, Tina never argued...never pushed. "What she looks like has nothing to do with her teaching or housekeeping skills."

"My point exactly."

"What are you implying?"

Her soft sigh came clearly across the wires. "I just want to know what type of woman is caring for my daughter."

"Meredith is very caring, very gentle, and a darn good teacher. Holly is interested in schoolwork for the first time in a long time."

"She sounds like a paragon," Tina muttered sarcastically, and loud enough for him to hear.

He stayed silent.

"I want Holly to come to New York in August as we originally planned."

"No way!"

"Cooper, you're being unreasonable about this."

"*I* have custody, Tina, because you didn't want it. It would have tied you down too much, you said. You would be doing publicity tours, traveling to L.A. The one thing we did agree on was that Holly was better off here with me.''

"But I want to see her!"

"The last time she visited you, you subjected her to a life-style that almost took her life. If she hadn't gone to that party with you, she would never have been hurt in the accident!"

"I'm her mother, Cooper. I deserve to see her."

"Then come here. Make enough time in your busy schedule to give her your undivided attention."

"I'll sue you for custody." Her words carried a serious warning.

"Try it," he returned. "*You* walked out. *You* abandoned your daughter. Just how do you think a judge will look at *that?*"

"It's not black-and-white, Cooper. And you don't hold all the cards. After all, you're living with a woman now."

"I am *not*—" but he realized his words had fallen on empty space. His ex-wife had cut the connection.

As he stood at the sink, anger with Tina an almost living thing in his chest, Meredith opened the door and stepped inside. She took one look at him and asked, "Do you want me to stay or go? I was going to make lunch."

He tightened his hands into fists, as if the motion could somehow squeeze the anger out. "My ex-wife just threatened to sue me for custody of Holly. The *last* thing on my mind is lunch." The vehemence of his tone carried the same intensity as his clenched fists.

But instead of beating a retreat as he expected, Meredith asked, "A stiff glass of Scotch instead?"

"Did you bring a bottle in your duffel bag?" he returned, admiring her ability to stand her ground and do it with dignity.

"No. Will anything else help?" She came a few steps closer.

"Yes. Somebody making Tina see what she did to Holly."

"Or what she did to you?"

He shook his head. "This isn't about me."

"Isn't it mostly about you?"

"You know nothing about it," he answered curtly, wishing she had gone back outside.

"I know about divorce. And the pain. And I know if you don't let go of it, it will take over your life."

This woman, who was only an arm's length away, who invaded his dreams, who aroused him by her mere presence, held up truth like a mirror. "I don't want your advice any more than I know what to do with the anger."

Meredith reached out and took his hand, holding his fist in her palm. "Let it go."

She was calm and softness, a gentle rain on parched earth. "Meredith..."

Covering the top of his fist with her other hand, she repeated, "Let at least some of it go."

Her green eyes mesmerized him as much as her touch, and something deep inside of him started releasing as he opened his fingers. "Tina says she'll sue, but she doesn't even *want* custody. She wants to be a mom when it's convenient for her! She walked out on us as if we didn't matter, as if fame and money were the only things she ever wanted."

His voice lowered a register as he shook his head. "When I was a kid and heard my parents fighting night after night, I promised myself I'd have a perfect marriage. No fights. The same values. Putting our children's lives before ours. But after Holly was born, Tina put off having more children. She started writing. She shut me out. And then she left without looking back, on an adventure she'd dreamed about all her life. I never even knew it was one of her dreams until it was too late!''

He'd never put it into words before, and doing it now led him to wonder what kind of magic Meredith Preston possessed that the regret had spurted out like a geyser.

"I'm sorry, Cooper."

He pulled his hand back, chagrined he'd put his emotion into Meredith's hands. "I don't want your pity."

"What *do* you want?"

"Breathing space. I can't seem to find it anymore. Especially when you're in the same room." If he kissed her again, the passion could sweep all other emotion away. Suddenly he needed the passion even more than he needed breathing space.

But as he reached out to pull Meredith into his arms, Holly came rushing up the porch and in the door, bringing him back to reality with a jolt. "I have a *great* idea," she announced. "Can Meredith come with us to the strawberry festival tomorrow?"

Cooper took a step back and a deep breath. "Meredith deserves a day off, small stuff."

His daughter tugged on Meredith's arm. "Please, will you come? You don't have to cook or clean or do schoolwork with me tomorrow. Does she, Dad? We can just have fun."

"It's up to Meredith," he said evenly, hoping she'd choose to do anything rather than spend the day with him and his daughter. The chemistry between them could suck him into deep trouble.

His gaze collided with hers as he waited for her decision.

Chapter Five

Just what would Cooper look like when he was having fun? Meredith wondered. Would the somber sparks in his eyes turn into amused twinkles? Would the hard set of his jaw soften? Would his stance become more relaxed, less militant in protection of his daughter and his values?

Curiosity and a deepening longing to know him better led her to smile at Holly. "I'd love to come along. I've never been to a strawberry festival. Where is it held?"

"Out by the lake," Holly answered. "Tell her, Dad. About the strawberry sundaes and waffles and pony rides and dancing on the lake."

"Dancing on the lake?" she repeated.

Cooper rubbed his jaw. "They string lanterns around the dock, and after dark there's music."

"It sounds like a terrific way to spend a day." She couldn't help imagining dancing with Cooper, being held in his arms.

"Oh, goody." Holly clapped her hands. "You can help us count the strawberries. Dad's always *way* off."

"Excuse me, young lady, but last year we almost won."

"Dad! There were ten guesses better than ours."

Cooper laughed. "That's the best we've ever done." With a smile still twitching at the corners of his mouth, he explained, "One of the farms loads a truck with baskets of strawberries. Whoever's guess is the closest to the actual number wins a five-hundred-dollar gift certificate from the chamber of commerce."

"Someone actually *counts* the strawberries?" Meredith asked.

"The number is in a sealed envelope the mayor carries around all day." Cooper's smile said this was indeed an important aspect of the festival.

"Well, I *am* pretty good at math," Meredith teased. "What time does the festival start?"

"Around ten. But we'll go to church first, then get lunch at the festival."

"Wanna come to church with us?" Holly asked Meredith.

Meredith had never been a regular churchgoer, but she suspected Cooper rarely missed a Sunday. When she glanced at him, he seemed to be waiting for her answer. "I'd like to go with you."

With a beaming smile, Holly went to Meredith and hugged her. "It'll be a great day. I'm gonna check the kittens."

After Holly had headed for the stairs, Meredith realized how dear the little girl was becoming to her. But when her gaze came to rest on Cooper, his expression was decidedly neutral. "Do you mind if I come along?" she asked him.

"Mind? I'm not sure how to answer that, Meredith. Holly wants you to come along, and I want to see her happy. As far as I'm concerned, this…chemistry between us is damn distracting. But maybe if we count strawberries together, it will go away.''

She suspected the opposite was true for her.

Only time would tell where a strawberry festival could lead them.

The day couldn't have been sunnier, the air fresher, the sky bluer. A strawberry breeze seemed to float around Meredith as Holly held her hand and tugged her from one booth to another. Cooper patiently stood by as she bought a jar of strawberry preserves and an apron trimmed in red with a large strawberry embroidered on the bib. With Cooper smiling down at her, his brown eyes amused, she wanted a memento of the day.

"Do women have a shopping gene that men are missing?" he teased as she picked up a pair of strawberry-dotted oven mitts.

She tipped her chin up. "Can you walk through a hardware store without seeing something you need?"

He grinned. "Touché."

Although Cooper had been serious as they'd attended the church service and appeared uncomfortable when he introduced her to one of his store employees and another neighbor who'd also attended the service, he was relaxed now. And yet…

He was careful not to come too close and to keep Holly between them. After they'd eaten cheese steak sandwiches, French fries and strawberry sundaes for lunch, they walked around the dock area, watching people navigate paddle boats. The sun sparkled and danced on the blue-green water. But Holly turned away from the lake, then tugged on Meredith's elbow.

As Meredith leaned down, Holly pointed to a sign in the distance. Pony Rides.

Holly's large brown eyes told Meredith the eight-year-old wanted her help. But Holly had to learn to ask her dad for what she wanted and needed herself. "Ask," she suggested close to the little girl's ear.

Holly frowned and Meredith encouragingly laid a hand on her shoulder.

"Dad?"

Cooper faced his daughter.

She pointed to the sign. "Can I go on a pony ride? Please?"

"Holly…"

"You won't let me ride Gypsy, but real *little* kids are riding the ponies. Please? I promise I'll just sit still and hold on."

Cooper's gaze fell on Meredith. She bet he didn't want her opinion, but he had agreed to listen to it. "It's something Holly really wants to do and probably one of the main reasons she wanted to come."

Holly nodded.

When Cooper didn't respond immediately, Meredith added, "The owner might even let you lead her yourself."

"This is a conspiracy," he grumbled. Then he flicked Holly's ponytail from her shoulder. "Okay, small stuff. Let's go stand in line, and I'll check out the temperament of the ponies."

As Meredith stood with Holly watching the children already mounted and riding around the enclosed area, Cooper spoke with the man in charge. A few minutes later he came over to his daughter and took her hand. "Let's get in line. Archie, over there, said I can lead you around myself."

Holly practically bounced with excitement as they

found the end of the line in back of a man who was as tall as Cooper and holding a toddler. When the dark-haired man saw Cooper, he grinned. "The best dads know the best places to bring their kids."

Cooper chuckled. "How are you doing, Daniel? Hi there, Susie. Are you going to ride a pony?"

When the little girl nodded, her brown curls bobbed across her cheeks. But after a shy smile at Cooper, she turned her face into her dad's shoulder.

Meredith watched as Daniel leaned his jaw briefly against his daughter's hair, and she knew he was a loving father.

"I missed you at the chamber of commerce meeting last week," Daniel said to Cooper.

"I've been trying to finish special orders that have stacked up."

When Daniel glanced at Holly's hand in Meredith's, Cooper introduced her. "Meredith Preston, this is Daniel Baxter. He owns the best home-improvement store in Harmony Hollow and another in Nashua. Meredith is tutoring Holly for the summer and keeping the house in order."

Daniel shook hands with Meredith. His grip was as strong as he was handsome, with his crooked smile and deep green eyes. But her pulse didn't speed up, nor did she feel any sensation other than the genuine friendliness offered. "It's good to meet you," he said.

Meredith smiled at Susie. "How old is your daughter?"

"Susie's two."

Suddenly the line moved, and it was Susie's turn to ride.

"Maybe I'll see you later. Are we still on for basketball next Saturday?" Daniel asked Cooper as he carried his daughter to a palomino pony.

Cooper called after him. "Sure are. I'll meet you at the school at one. Are you going to remind Jake?"

Daniel settled his little girl in the saddle and called back, "I'll make a point of it."

As Susie's pony moved forward, and she smiled and held on tightly to the pommel, Cooper said to Meredith, "He's had a rough time of it. His wife died about a year ago."

"Does he care for Susie himself?"

"His mother-in-law takes care of her."

As another pony became free, Cooper said, "C'mon, small stuff. It's your turn."

Holly couldn't contain her excitement as Cooper helped her into the saddle. She held the reins but waved at Meredith often as she rode around the fenced-in area, a wide grin from ear to ear.

When the ride was over, it came as no surprise to Meredith that Holly looked up at Cooper and asked, "Can I ride Gypsy now? Please? Even if you just walk her around the paddock?"

Cooper crouched down beside his daughter. "You think if I say yes you'll be riding Gypsy alone again by the end of the week. That's not going to happen, Holly."

Her smile faded. "But you will let me ride if you walk her?"

Glancing up at Meredith, he gave her a wry grin. "I can't think of a good reason not to."

Holly wrapped her arms around his neck and squeezed him hard. "Thank you, Daddy."

By the way Cooper hugged his daughter and closed his eyes, Meredith knew he was fighting emotion. After a few moments he stood and cleared his throat. "Let's go count those strawberries."

As they pitched Ping-Pong balls to try to win goldfish,

watched a gymnastics performance and fed ducks leftover waffles, Meredith marveled at the many people Cooper knew.

Relaxed, without the wariness Meredith usually felt emanating from him, Cooper explained how Harmony Hollow was once a farming community until businesses sprung up to subsidize the farms, and housing developments overtook fertile fields. Now industry, business and farming worked together to create community spirit in the midsize town. As a duck stole a bite of waffle from Meredith's fingers, Alma Macavee walked up to where they sat under a tall sycamore.

Smiling, she asked, "Tuckered out already?"

Cooper stood. "Just enjoying the day before we head back. It's time for Holly to rest."

"Aw, Dad…"

Alma chuckled. "I'm on my way home for a rest myself. Are you coming back tonight to see if you won the strawberry count?"

"I don't think so…"

"Dad, you *have* to," Holly protested as she scrambled to her feet. "And if you don't come back you'll miss the dancing. Maybe Mrs. Macavee can stay with me for a little…"

Cooper's frown said he didn't want to impose on Alma for something he considered unimportant. But the older woman patted his arm. "That's a fine idea. I'll bring my knitting with me, and Holly can read me some of her books."

Looking disconcerted, Cooper glanced at Meredith. "Would you like to come back this evening?"

"It sounds like fun," she responded, as if spending time alone with him didn't matter.

"All right, Alma. We'll take you up on your offer."

Her blue eyes twinkled. "I'll be over around seven."

Cupping his daughter's chin, Cooper asked her, "And why are you so determined for me to come dancing?"

"Because you haven't had any fun since Mom left…and Meredith is nice."

Meredith felt her cheeks redden as she stood and brushed off her jeans, avoiding Cooper's gaze.

Cooper curved his arm around Holly's shoulders. "Okay, I promise you I'll have fun tonight. Now let's go buy some fresh strawberries to take along home."

As Meredith came up beside Holly, her eyes met Cooper's. He'd been forced into a "date" of sorts and she wondered how his idea of fun compared to hers!

Meredith's simplest clothes hung in the closet in Cooper's guest room. She tucked in the turquoise peasant blouse and straightened the band on the matching dirndl skirt. The designer label brushed her finger, reminding her of the world she'd left behind in Pennsylvania. She'd settled in so easily here, surprising herself. Determined to teach Holly and do a good job of it, she'd never expected to actually enjoy cooking for Cooper and his daughter, doing laundry, taking care of them.

Admit it, Meredith. This is more than a job.

As she slipped her feet into a pair of flat white-leather shoes, she was afraid to admit it. What if Cooper knew about her former life in Pennsylvania? That she didn't *have* to work? That her trust fund and divorce settlement were enough security for more than one lifetime?

There was no reason to tell Cooper.

Was she afraid of his reaction as well as her deepening feelings for him?

Fear wasn't new to Meredith. She remembered the nights filled with it after her mother died, after her father remarried, when she'd started having cramps and lost her babies. But she knew there was only one way to shatter fear, and that was to march directly into the face of it.

Except this time…

The risks seemed greater. It wasn't just her and Cooper. Holly was involved, too.

Yet wasn't finding true love worth the risk? For all of them?

She thought about Luke and Becca. They'd come from two different worlds and merged their lives perfectly. Smiling when she thought of the happiness her stepsister and brother-in-law shared, she applied a soft sheen of lipstick to her lips, grabbed her sweater and opened her door.

When she passed Holly's room, she saw her sitting on her bed, already dressed in her nightgown. The kittens lay sleeping beside her.

"Are you going to pick out books to read to Mrs. Macavee?"

Holly nodded.

Meredith was getting to know this child pretty well, and she could tell something was wrong. "Would you like me and your dad to stay home tonight?"

"No! It's just…my leg hurts. Not a whole lot but—"

"You walked quite a bit today. Why don't I massage it for you? That might help."

"Miss Nancy does that sometimes if I work real hard."

Meredith smiled. "I've watched her. Let me go get my lotion."

A few minutes later Meredith was sitting on Holly's bed, soothing and kneading Holly's leg. When her thumbs passed over the scars, Holly's gaze held hers. "Do you think the kids will make fun of me when I go back to school?"

Meredith could see that Holly wanted the truth. "I think

your limp is less noticeable just in the past two weeks. If you keep working hard till September, it might be gone.''

''And I can wear jeans to school to hide the scars.''

Massaging around Holly's knee, Meredith responded, ''You can. But then what happens the first time you want to wear a skirt?''

When Holly frowned, she looked troubled. ''But if I don't cover them, kids might point and laugh.''

''*Or* you could explain exactly what happened, not pay them any mind and everyone will follow your example.''

''Really?''

''Meredith's right.'' Cooper's deep voice came from the doorway. ''Is your leg hurting?''

''It feels better now.''

At Cooper's arched brows, Holly reassured him. ''Honest it does. Meredith made it feel better. Is Mrs. Macavee here yet?''

''She just arrived.''

''I want to show her the kittens. Can I take them downstairs?''

''Go on down. I'll bring them in the box.''

Holly found her slippers and with a grin went downstairs.

''Do you think we should stay home?'' he asked, his gaze assessing Meredith as it passed over her blouse and skirt.

''I think she'll be fine for a while. She overused muscles today. I can give her another massage if she's uncomfortable when we get back. I think she feels guilty for all the care you've had to give her.''

''It's not *her* fault.''

''No, but she's a smart little girl. She knows your work is backed up. And apparently she thinks you don't have fun anymore.'' The last she said with a teasing smile, hoping to coax one from him.

He towered over her, his gaze unwavering. He'd changed clothes after supper. This morning, he'd looked handsome and sexy in the suit and tie he'd worn to church. This afternoon in his usual blue jeans and T-shirt, she'd been all too aware of his muscular physique. Tonight, dressed in a cream collarless shirt and black jeans, he looked like a man who was confident in who he was, no matter what he wore. And he was still too sexy for her peace of mind.

When he didn't respond, she snapped the lid on the lotion and stood. But he didn't move away. She was close enough to feel his body heat.

''You look very pretty tonight,'' he murmured, his gaze falling on her lips.

Her throat suddenly went very dry and all she could manage was a brief, ''Thank you.''

''Are you ready?'' he asked, the brown of his eyes deepening.

Ready to go back to the strawberry festival? Ready to dance with him? Ready to kiss him again? *All of the above,* she decided with a certain ''Yes.''

''Don't forget your sweater,'' he reminded gently with a nod to it on the bed. ''The night air will be cool.'' A moment later he'd scooped the kittens into the box and left the room.

Cooper definitely upset her equilibrium. Maybe tonight she could figure out why she was starting not to mind.

The crowd at Harmony Lake had thinned considerably as Cooper and Meredith returned to the strawberry festival. Meredith could hear music as soon as she alighted from Cooper's truck in the immense parking lot. Walking beside him, she realized he'd slowed his pace to match hers. He was a thoughtful man, yet still very on guard, still very angry at what had happened to his marriage…and to Holly. But maybe tonight, for a little while, he could forget the anger and let down the guard.

A breeze blew across the lake as they approached the dock. Meredith swung her sweater around her shoulders, but it slipped and Cooper caught it. When he held it for her, she slid her arm into one sleeve, aware of his tall body behind her, very close. As she slid her arm into the second sleeve, his fingers brushed her hair and grazed her neck. She knew if she glanced over her shoulder, her cheek would probably meet his chest. He'd used a spicy cologne that made her think of tall ships and pirates and a man carrying away his lady in his arms. Since when had she entertained such romantic fantasies?

Since the first moment she'd laid eyes on Cooper.

After she straightened her sweater and turned, Cooper was still very close. The music playing on the dock a mere fifty feet away was slow and moody. An electric organ, guitar and saxophone melded under the blue, green and yellow lights to create a separate world for the dancers on the dock.

"They're supposed to announce the winner around eight," Cooper said, his voice deep and husky. "Would you like to dance until they do?"

When she lifted her chin, her gaze met his. "Yes."

His arm slid around her until his hand rested in the small of her back, guiding her toward the lights and music. Her heart raced in anticipation of being held in his arms. What should she say? How should she act? Was he here because of Holly's suggestion or because he wanted to dance with her?

Cooper greeted at least three people he knew as he

found them an empty space on the dock. "I haven't done this for a while, so your feet could be in danger," he warned her with a crooked grin as he took her hand and drew her into a traditional dance embrace.

"I'll keep that in mind," she answered as her hand on his shoulder could feel the heat of his body through his shirt.

They danced in silence until Meredith decided conversation would be easier to deal with than the keen awareness of every inch of his hard body. "When was the last time you danced?" she asked.

Cooper's guidance was firm and sure with no hesitation. "Tina got a call from her agent that she'd sold her first book. I took her to Manchester to celebrate."

His deliberately even tone told Meredith she might have opened Pandora's box, but if she wanted to know Cooper, she needed to know more about him. "Have you dated since your divorce?"

For a moment she thought he was going to tell her to mind her own business. But then he shook his head. "I haven't had time. When I'm not working, I'm taking care of Holly. How about you?"

Men had asked her, from tennis partners at her fitness club to fellow students on campus where she'd earned her degree. But she'd turned them all down, not wanting either a casual relationship *or* one that could hurt her again. "After my divorce, I focused on earning my degree." Deciding she needed to be honest with Cooper, she added, "It was safer."

His brown eyes studied her, then he confessed, "I know exactly what you mean."

The cool breeze lifted her hair and tossed a strand across her cheek. Before she could brush it away, Cooper released her hand and reached for it himself. His index finger traced the curve of the tendril very close to her lips. She trembled from the touch of his skin on hers and closed her eyes so he couldn't see how he was affecting her. But after he brushed the strand away, his finger grazed the line of her lower lip.

"Look at me, Meredith."

When she opened her eyes, she saw the desire in his and took a deep breath.

"We're playing with fire. You realize that, don't you?"

Her voice had deserted her and all she could do was nod.

With a low groan, he took her hand again, tucked it into his chest and held her close. His thighs pressed against hers as he guided her to the music, and she could feel the strong beat of his heart.

When his jaw brushed her temple, she looked up and saw desire and male hunger in his eyes. Was she ready for it? Or had she made a mistake coming here with him, melting in his arms like this....

The music stopped, and a man in a suit stepped up to the microphone. Everyone else was dressed casually, and he stood out, but not only because of the suit. As Cooper released her, she took a deep breath and tried to slow her racing pulse. Avoiding Cooper's gaze, she turned toward the man at the mike. He had striking black hair and serious blue eyes. But he smiled at the dancers and said, "The mayor insisted I should announce our winner."

"That's Jacob Chandler," Cooper said close to her ear. "He owns Chandler Enterprises on the south side of town and funds a chunk of the strawberry festival each year."

As Cooper's deep voice vibrated near her cheek and his hand still rested at the small of her back, she almost missed Jacob Chandler's announcement.

"The winner of the strawberry festival's traditional count-the-strawberries contest is…Alma Macavee."

Cooper laughed. "Good for her!" Then he called, "Jake, Alma's not here tonight."

Jake waved, signaling that he'd heard. Into the mike he said, "I've been informed Mrs. Macavee isn't here. I'll deliver this to her tomorrow. The music will continue until eleven so enjoy yourselves. I'd like to thank everyone in Harmony for making the strawberry festival a success again. The vendors voted unanimously to donate 10 percent of their proceeds this year to the new children's wing at the hospital."

Applause broke out and continued until Jake held up a hand. "If any of you would like to make a donation, just contact me at Chandler Enterprises and I'll give you the information you need. Enjoy the rest of the evening."

As Jake left the microphone and made his way through the crowd, several people stopped him.

"Jake always could get a job done and done well," Cooper said.

"You know him?"

"We went to high school together, Daniel Baxter, too. Jake moved away after college and made a name for himself buying declining companies and turning them around. He moved his headquarters here a couple of years ago."

"You admire him," she commented.

"I've always admired him. He's made a lot of money, but he treats his friends as if we're all still in high school. We get together to play basketball once a month and go for a beer."

The band began to play an old-fashioned waltz. When Cooper arched his brows in invitation and Meredith nodded, he took her in his arms and swept her into the music as if they'd been dancing together for years. And when the waltz ended, she felt breathless, fully alive, anticipating whatever else the night would bring. As the music started up again, this time the song was slow and sultry. Cooper closed the more proper distance between them, drawing Meredith into his chest as if she belonged there.

The lights seemed to dim, the music seemed to fade, the other couples seemed to no longer exist. As the breeze whispered over the lake, Meredith melted deeper into Cooper's arms. When he guided her toward a darker corner of the dock, she followed him, led by instinct, romance and the moonlight. Their dance steps became a slow sway; the music became a rhythm that bound them together.

It came as no surprise to Meredith when Cooper released her hand, wrapped both strong arms around her and locked his hands at her waist. Reflexively she reached around his neck, her breasts against his chest, her hands tempted by the hair at his nape. When she gazed up at him, his eyes settled on her mouth and the anticipation of the entire evening coalesced into a kiss.

Starting out easy, Cooper simply brushed his lips back and forth over hers, taunting them both. She could feel the tension stringing his body tighter, the arousal he didn't attempt to hide. He honestly desired her and wanted her to know it. When his tongue playfully danced across her lower lip, her breath caught. An excitement she'd never known swirled in her tummy and made her legs weak. With Cooper holding her tight, she simply enjoyed the sensation.

As Cooper opened his mouth over hers, she laced her hands in his hair, breathed in the scent of spice and Cooper, and gave herself up to the intoxication of the moment. His tongue was erotic, demanding, searching for her desire and coaxing it to match his. She didn't need any coaxing. With her body pressed tightly against his, the pleasure they could give each other was blatantly apparent. In all her married years, she'd never felt this heat sweeping over her, the deep yearning to be joined to this man. Had she changed so much? Had she denied herself pleasure for so long that the idea of it was overwhelming her now? Or did her growing feelings for Cooper make her want differently, more intensely?

Cooper ended the kiss, only to brush his lips across her cheek, to play with her earlobe with his tongue, to murmur in her ear, "Let's take this someplace more private."

Suddenly the breeze from the lake became a cold wind, and she shivered. Cooper wanted to have sex with her.

Hadn't her ex-husband proved men thought about sex differently from women?

When she'd been caught up in grief after her second miscarriage, Brian hadn't known how to hold her, how to comfort her, how to reassure her that they'd make it through together. He'd wanted his needs met. And he wasn't willing to wait for her to heal. So he'd found someone else to meet his needs and have his babies.

She'd been foolish to think she could come here with Cooper tonight...

Leaning back, she studied his face, the deep character lines, the determined jaw, the sexy beard shadow evident even in the dusk. Did he feel more than desire? She had to know, and there was only one place to start. "Cooper, are you still in love with Tina?"

Chapter Six

When Cooper abruptly released Meredith and stepped back, she suspected he was angry as well as frustrated. His words proved it.

"You have no right to ask," he answered sharply.

But Meredith cared too much about him already to let him shut her out. "When a man kisses a woman like you just kissed me, I think she has some rights."

The night shadows played across his features as he fought emotions he obviously was keeping under wraps. His eyes and his expression never gave anything away unless he wanted them to. But in the short time she'd been around him, she'd learned to read the subtle signals: his brown irises widened; his jaw tilted; his lips firmed into a taut line.

"Rights or expectations?" His hard tone said he didn't like the idea of her either wanting rights or having expectations.

"I'm not sure. If you answer my question, maybe we'll both find out."

He swore, then snapped, "I am *not* in love with my ex-wife."

"You obviously still have strong feelings about her."

"I wouldn't have any feelings at all if it weren't for Holly. Tina killed anything I felt the day she walked out. I can understand how she could leave *me,* but not Holly."

"I can't understand that, either," Meredith said softly. "When a woman carries a child…" Tears welled up from emotions past and present, and she blinked them away. "Do you know what I would give to have a child, to cherish a child, to love a child?"

His expression gentled. "Not all women see motherhood the same way."

"Maybe there are different degrees."

"Being a parent is all or nothing, Meredith. Fascinated with her new life, Tina forgot that fact one evening, and look what happened."

"You can't be at odds with her the rest of your days."

"I can be at odds with her if it protects Holly." He gazed down at her under the colored lights. "But Tina has nothing to do with what happened here tonight. It's chemistry, plain and simple, and you're afraid of it."

Just as she thought. Cooper's explanation for his desire was due to hormones. Hers was a lot more complicated. "Sex is never plain and simple, Cooper. Not for most women. Certainly not for me. Yes, I do think I have rights. And if I make love with a man, I have expectations, too, that there's a strong bond between us…a commitment. I didn't come to Harmony Hollow for a fling that's going to put another hole in my heart."

As the silence lengthened, his eyes narrowed. "Then stay away from me, Meredith. A commitment is the last thing I'm looking for. I thought we could share a little pleasure, make the earth spin for a few moments, forget about aching hearts.''

Pride straightened her shoulders and added crispness to her voice. "I won't have a problem staying away from you, Cooper. I've had practice dealing with men who believe their hearts and bodies function separately." Then she turned and left him standing on the dock, just wanting to reach the darkness of his truck without making a bigger fool of herself than she already had. She'd nip her feelings for Cooper in the bud and concentrate on Holly. That's why she'd come to Harmony Hollow.

The sun beat down on the schoolyard's asphalt Saturday morning as Jake tossed the basketball to Cooper and it slid right through his hands. When he swore and chased it a couple of steps, Jake called, "That's the second time I've caught you sleeping. What's wrong?"

Cooper dribbled the ball and passed it to Daniel.

"Nothing's wrong."

With arched brows, Daniel exchanged a look with Jake. "I think his preoccupation has something to do with Holly's teacher. He *did* tell you there's a beautiful blonde living under his roof, didn't he?"

Straightening, Jake pushed his black hair off his forehead with his wristband. "The same blonde you were dancing with on the dock?"

"Thanks, Daniel," Cooper mumbled.

"What are friends for?" Daniel asked with a grin.

After a move as quick and lethal as a panther's, Jake stole the ball from Cooper. "What gives, pal?"

With a grunt of exasperation, Cooper crossed to the chain-link fence surrounding the schoolyard and yanked his towel from the post. As he wiped his face, he tried to sort his thoughts about Meredith. That kiss, the disappointment in her eyes when he'd told her he was only interested in sex, had thrown him more than he wanted to admit. For the past week they'd barely spoken to each other except when Holly was around.

He didn't know what he'd expected. After all, he'd told her to stay away from him. Tact had never been his strong suit, and he shouldn't have been so blunt. He should have been—

Geez. The truth was that being under the same roof with Meredith, whether she was treating him like a stranger or kissing him back, kept him in a tailspin. He didn't understand his reaction to her. He'd never felt such an upheaval around Tina, even when he'd courted her. Settling down with her had been a rational decision. He'd wanted a wife and had chosen one. He'd wanted a family so they'd started one. Then Tina left.

This thing with Meredith…

There *was* nothing with Meredith. For a while on the dock he'd imagined mutual pleasure, physical satisfaction for as long as she stayed. But she'd nixed that idea, and he couldn't give more.

Did Daniel's and Jake's expectant expressions annoy him because there *was* something to tell or because there *wasn't?* He'd keep it simple. "Because of the accident, Holly has a lot of schoolwork to catch up on. Because of taking care of her, I have orders backed up. Meredith Preston is tutoring Holly and taking care of the house."

"Like a nanny?" Jake asked.

"You could say that." Cooper took another swipe at his neck with his towel.

"And?" his friend pressed.

"And nothing. She's leaving at the end of the summer."

"Is she from around here?" Jake asked.

"Pennsylvania. So...now that I gave you the scoop, can we play ball?"

"I think there's something at the bottom of that scoop. I didn't leave right away Saturday night, and I saw you two find a dark corner. I figured you were finally realizing there are women beyond Tina," Jake remarked.

Silence hummed until Cooper blew out a breath. "All right. Meredith's got looks. I'm attracted to her. But she's not the type of woman who wants a summer fling."

"Said no, did she?" Jake asked with a sly smile.

"Jake..." Daniel warned.

Cooper knew that Jake's divorce had left him cynical and distrustful of women. Daniel had always been more diplomatic. Both of them had been good friends over the years. "You want the truth?" Cooper asked. "I would have taken her to bed, but like I said, she's not the type for a one-night stand. End of story. *Now* can we get back to the game?"

Jake shook his head. "The end of summer is weeks away. I have a feeling you're going to be taking lots of cold showers."

Slapping his towel over the fence, Cooper moved fast and knocked the basketball out of Jake's hands. He dribbled, aimed and shot. When the ball bounced off the backboard, Jake and Daniel ran in for the rebound.

But Cooper caught the ball and sank it.

There was no reason he couldn't live under the same roof with an attractive woman and control his sexual urges—no reason at all.

Murphy's Furniture was situated in the center of town on a side street that ran parallel to the main thoroughfare. Meredith pulled into a spot in the asphalt parking lot, surprised at the number of cars parked there on a Monday morning. Then she saw the large red Summer Sale sign in the plate-glass window and realized she probably hadn't been able to get through to Cooper by phone because of the sale.

It had been over a week since she'd left him standing on the dock. Over a week of ignoring the deep baritone of his voice, his pensive gaze, the vibrations that still hummed between them even though they were both denying them. She'd only talked to him about Holly. When Holly was around, she conversed with him about his daughter's activities, schoolwork, physical therapy...or the weather. She never got close enough that any part of them touched.

She'd taken yesterday off again and explored the sights in the area, returning late last night following a movie. After she'd said a cursory good-night to Cooper, she'd peeked in on Holly and the kittens who had been to the vet for shots and an exam and now had the run of her room. After she'd gone to bed, she couldn't sleep. Cooper too often invaded her dreams. And when she heard his footfalls in the hall around midnight, she couldn't keep her heart from wishing they could at least be friends.

"Do you really think Dad will let us go rock hunting?" Holly asked as she unfastened her seat belt.

"Let's go find out. If he doesn't, we can pull the weeds that have already sprung up in the garden and see if any of our vegetables are coming up." In the plot Cooper had tilled for them, they'd planted carrots, radishes, tomatoes and garden lettuce. She and Holly had also planted petunias, pansies and snapdragons in the front yard. Science was much more fun when it was hands-on.

When Meredith stepped into Murphy's Furniture, customers were milling about, waiting for members of Cooper's sales force who were already busy.

"I'll go see if Dad's in his office," Holly said, and took off for the back of the store.

Meredith decided to wait in the showroom and look around Cooper's store. As she approached a living room grouping, a customer sitting on the sofa with a fabric booklet looked up and smiled. "Can I ask your opinion about something?"

When Meredith and her ex-husband had moved into a house, she'd done the decorating herself. She'd always loved mixing and matching colors, fabrics and textures. So now she answered the woman with a smile of her own. "Sure."

The customer asked, "Which fabric do you think goes better with this sofa?"

Meredith sat down beside her.

The week-long sale always brought a flurry of customers to the store. Cooper had just finished writing up a special order and was placing the sales slip in his office when he saw Holly standing at the door.

"Hi, there, small stuff. Is something wrong?"

"Nope. Me and Meredith want to ask you somethin' and the line's been busy for the past hour."

Cooper glanced at the receptionist, who was on the phone fielding questions about the ads that had run in the Sunday paper. "Where is Meredith?"

"Out front. She's looking around."

Meredith was still being civil, politely friendly whenever Holly was around, distant when she wasn't. It was driving him nuts. Yet he couldn't come up with a viable alternative that didn't include taking Meredith to bed. Jake had been right about the cold showers.

Switching his attention to his daughter, he smiled at her. "What did you want to ask me?"

"Can we go on a rock hunt out at the lake? Meredith said she saw all kinds there when we were feeding the ducks."

Cooper was beginning to feel confident in Meredith's ability to care for Holly. She made sure she checked with him before they did anything out of the ordinary. "Do you want to go?"

"You bet! Meredith said we might be able to get a rock-polishing kit and make paperweights, maybe even jewelry. Wouldn't that be cool?"

More and more often "Meredith said" had crept into Holly's recitations of their day-to-day activities.

"I suppose that could be cool. C'mon. Let's find Meredith."

When Cooper spotted her, he was struck again by her classic beauty. Her pink cotton blouse and jeans made her features even more refined. He was surprised to see her talking animatedly with one of his customers, Mrs. Barlow. The talkative woman with the stiffly sprayed, frosted hair always took forever to make up her mind, asking for advice from anyone and everyone within shouting distance. Now, as she saw him approaching, she beckoned to him with a smile.

Before he could even greet her, she began, "You *must* hire this young woman. She knows exactly what goes with what, which colors work best. Instead of the plain fabric, I'm getting the sofa in the floral and the chair with a small stripe in a complementary color, of course. Can you take my order?"

He couldn't believe Mrs. Barlow had decided that quickly. When he glanced at Meredith, she gave a small shrug.

"Mrs. Barlow, if you give me a minute, I'll be right with you," he said.

When his customer nodded, he motioned Meredith and Holly to the side. Meredith's green gaze collided with his, and he almost forgot what he was going to say.

"So…Dad. Can we go?" Holly asked.

Breaking eye contact with Meredith, he remembered Holly's request. "You can go rock hunting if you stay away from the water."

"Aw, Dad…"

"That's my condition, Holly," he concluded in a firm tone.

"Okay," she replied with a patient sigh. "But can I ride Gypsy tonight?"

Holly was becoming very good at negotiating. "All right. But I want you to rest for a while this afternoon, and that doesn't mean playing with the kittens."

She thought about it for a moment. "It's a deal. Can I start bringing the kittens downstairs?"

"I suppose that means we'll need a litter box down there, too. I'll pick one up on my way home, and we can put it in the laundry room."

Holly grinned. "Thanks, Dad."

As his daughter headed for the store's front entrance and her day's adventure, Meredith assured him, "I won't let her overdo. I just thought some walking and the sunshine would be good for her."

He suddenly was gripped with a strong desire to talk to Meredith about something other than Holly, to kiss her as he'd kissed her on the dock even if it had nowhere to go. "I'm sure it will be."

After a moment of silence, Meredith murmured, "We'll get going and let you go back to work." When she would have turned away, he clasped her arm.

Her brows arched in surprise; her soft skin scalded him,

and he dropped his hand. "I just wanted to thank you for being patient with Mrs. Barlow."

"No thanks necessary. I've always liked mixing and matching furniture. If I can't find another teaching position at the end of summer, maybe I'll apply for a job at a furniture store."

Her green eyes twinkled, and he couldn't tell if she was serious or teasing him.

"Meredith, are you coming?" Holly called.

With one of her gentle smiles that seemed genuine rather than merely polite today, Meredith said, "I'll see you tonight."

As she walked away and joined his daughter at the door, he realized he didn't like the idea of her leaving at summer's end.

He didn't like it at all.

Planning meals was becoming easier for Meredith. Not only had she made friends with the butcher, but Holly's physical therapist had brought Meredith a few of her favorite recipes and recommended a good basic cookbook. Between the gourmet section of the supermarket and her imagination, vanilla ice cream topped with wild blueberry sauce became a fancy dessert.

When the phone rang, Meredith had just set a meat loaf in the oven beside foil-wrapped potatoes. She reached it on the third ring.

"Murphy residence," she answered, peering out the kitchen window at Holly, who was playing with the kittens by the swing in the back of the house.

"Hello. This is Holly's mother."

"Oh! Hello, Mrs.—"

"It's Ms. Dade. I use my maiden name. You must be Meredith."

"Yes."

"Holly talks about you every time I call. Cooper, on the other hand…"

"I'll get Holly, Ms. Dade."

"Meredith, wait. Uh, look. This is so awkward. I really miss my daughter. You're spending every day with her."

Meredith kept silent knowing that had been Tina's choice. Was she regretting it?

"I told Cooper I want her to spend some time with me in New York before school starts again, but he won't let her come see me. Maybe you could convince him."

"This is between you and Cooper."

"Not exactly. As fondly as Holly speaks of you, I'm sure you're fond of her, too."

"She's a terrific little girl."

"I love her and she loves me, no matter what Cooper has told you. Don't you think we need to spend some time together? Cooper wants me to come to Harmony Hollow. But Holly loves New York, and we always have such a good time…"

Meredith knew Tina was thinking of the accident. "Cooper does what he thinks is best for Holly."

"What's best is *not* keeping her in a protective bubble."

In some ways, Meredith knew Tina was right.

"Will you talk to him for me?"

"I don't know—"

"Please, Meredith. Just try. Talk to Holly, too. She wants to come. Maybe if you can get Cooper to see *her* point of view, he'll let her."

"Let me think about it. Ms.—"

"It's Tina. And thank you. I know you'll try to do what's best for Holly. Is she nearby?"

"I'll get her."

As Meredith pushed open the screen door, she wondered what she'd just gotten herself into.

Cooper's day had consisted of nonstop customers and one very unusual phone request. He was later than he planned getting home. He would have stayed at the store till closing at eight, but he'd promised Holly a ride on Gypsy and told himself his sales force could handle the customers. Meredith had taken his late homecoming in stride but had seemed preoccupied throughout supper. He needed to discuss something with her, anyway. Maybe he'd find out what was wrong.

After dessert, Holly went to the paddock to wait for him. Meredith took the stack of dessert plates to the sink, and he collected the remaining silverware. Opening the dishwasher, he said, "Mrs. Barlow called this afternoon."

"Did she change her mind?" Meredith asked.

"No. She spoke with a couple of her friends and they'd like to make an appointment with you so you can give them ideas on decorating."

"You're not serious!"

"Mrs. Barlow was very serious. I don't know what you said to her, but she was impressed. She says Harmony Hollow needs an interior decorating service. Apparently one of her friends wants to redecorate her bedroom and another a living room. Mrs. Barlow offered to pay you twenty-five dollars an hour for consultation, and they'd buy their furniture from me. She seemed to think that point alone would persuade me to convince you to go for this."

When Meredith pushed her hair behind her ear, Cooper recognized the gesture. She did it when she needed a few moments to think before she answered. Finally she said, "I'm flattered."

He waited.

"Would you like me to do this?" she asked, her green eyes cautious.

"The decision is yours, Meredith. I just told Mrs. Barlow I'd pass along her request."

"But it would help your business if I met with these women."

"Possibly. But I don't want you to feel pressured. I hired you to teach Holly, not sell furniture."

She smiled at him then. "I suppose there's no reason why I can't do both. Though I'd like to become familiar with the lines and fabrics you carry before I give Mrs. Barlow's friends any advice."

"Are you *sure* you want to do this?" He didn't want to take advantage of her or her time.

"Actually, it sounds like fun."

"You know, don't you, that if they like your ideas, they'll tell their friends. Clarice Barlow is the president of Harmony Hollow's gardening club. And she belongs to two bridge circles. These women could keep you busy for weeks," he said with some amusement.

Meredith laughed, and the lovely sound of it along with the picture of her standing at his sink tightened his chest.

"Then you'll make a tidy profit," she teased. "I'll call her and set something up."

The urge to kiss Meredith was so strong he took a deep breath and dropped the silverware in his hand into the rack in the dishwasher.

"Cooper, there's something I'd like to talk to you about," Meredith said, her voice serious.

Straightening, he guessed he was about to learn what had preoccupied her during supper. "Something you want to do with Holly?" His daughter had shown him a few of the rocks she'd found and chattered about what she'd learned while they'd eaten supper.

Meredith wiped her hands on a dish towel and faced him. "No." Again she pushed her hair behind her ear. "Tina called earlier."

He braced himself, expecting trouble. "And?"

"After she called, I had a long talk with Holly. Tina wanted me to ask you to consider how Holly feels about visiting her in New York. She misses her mother, Cooper. Will you reconsider letting her visit Tina in August?"

He didn't know if he was angrier at his ex-wife or Meredith. Tina had one thing on her mind—getting what she wanted. Meredith, on the other hand, knew exactly how he felt about this...why he was determined not to put his daughter in harm's way again. "You have no business meddling, Meredith. Holly isn't safe with Tina because Tina doesn't think of anyone but herself. A chauffeur-driven car, fancy jewelry, restaurants that charge more for dinner than normal families pay for groceries for a week will not make my daughter's life better."

"I don't know about better, Cooper. But experience can make life richer. If you keep letting your anger and fear color what you let Holly do, she's going to resent it. She's going to resent you for keeping her away from her mother!"

"In the long run, she'll thank me because I'm the one keeping her safe."

"She won't see it that way."

"And just how do *you* know?"

"I lost my mother. I know how it feels to miss that connection, the comfort, the knowing that she's there. If Holly doesn't think she can go to Tina when she needs her—"

"Don't put your feelings on my daughter. You have no

idea how Tina hurt Holly by leaving. *I'm* the one who has to wipe her tears, hold her after bad dreams, reassure her Tina still loves her when I'm not sure of that myself. My ex-wife broke promises and a little girl's heart. So don't you dare try to convince me Tina wants what's best for Holly when you obviously know nothing about that kind of pain.''

Anger spotted Meredith's cheeks. ''You don't have the market cornered on pain and betrayal.''

The need to touch her was so strong he couldn't resist, and he took her chin in his hand. ''Who betrayed you?''

Maybe it was the dare in his voice that she share something intimate, maybe it was the hunger in his touch, or maybe it was the memory of him telling her to stay away from him that made her pull out of his grasp and straighten her shoulders.

''Meredith...''

''You can't have it both ways, Cooper. Either you want me to keep my distance or you don't.''

''What if I just want to kiss you and hang the consequences?''

She tossed her towel onto the counter. ''I won't be a convenient nanny who—''

Impulsively he pulled her into his arms. A breath before his lips met hers, he murmured, ''You're anything but convenient.'' And before she could argue with him, his mouth opened over hers.

The kiss was as intimate as a kiss could get, as hot as a blazing firestorm. The taste of her had the power of aged brandy, intoxicating him before he realized it could. His arms shifted lower, bringing their differences closer together until neither could deny the perfect match. Meredith tightened her arms around him, signaling the same urgency he felt to take the kiss deeper, to let desire take its course, to forget about distance and fulfill each other's needs.

He possessed her for the moment, reveling in his ability to make her tongue chase after his, to draw soft murmurs from her throat, to urge her heartbeat to a speeding rate that matched his. When his hips moved against hers, she arched into him, and he groaned from the sheer pleasurable sensation.

His imagination conjured up erotic pictures that drove him on. Would she make love the same way she kissed? With the same sensual fire? With an abandon he'd never experienced from a woman? Would she act coy or shy or free?

He could tell the moment her thoughts wrapped themselves around her desire. In less than a heartbeat, she dropped her arms to her sides, broke free of the kiss and put a good six inches between them. His body ached to have her back in his arms, but he knew she'd resist. He wanted Meredith willing—no other way.

"Why did you do that?" she asked, her voice shaky but her green eyes shooting sparks.

"Why did *I* do that?" He wasn't about to take all the blame for a kiss he'd begun but she'd participated in as actively as he had.

Her face flushed pinker, and she looked as if she'd like to clobber him. "I don't understand you, Cooper. One minute you're telling me to stay away. The next—"

"It's simple, Meredith. I want you. And you want me."

"You don't want me. You want to take me to bed. There's a world of difference between the two."

"You weren't thinking much of the difference a minute ago."

"I wasn't thinking at all. I was feeling. Were you?"

He couldn't admit the emotions she stirred up or what they might mean to his life. "Oh, I was feeling, all right."

He'd never seen Meredith angry, but she was furious right now, and her glare should have brought him to his knees in apology. But he wouldn't apologize for the truth.

Abruptly Meredith untied her apron, yanked it over her head and flapped it on the counter. "I'm going for a walk. I'll finish cleaning this up later."

"Meredith…"

"If you don't want me leaving at sunup, you'd better not say another word."

He'd never abided threats or ultimatums, but he didn't want her to leave, for his sake as well as his daughter's. They both needed Meredith. He just wasn't ready to admit how or why.

So he kept silent as she crossed the kitchen and headed toward the foyer. And he pretended he didn't care as he heard the front door slam.

But as he went out back to find Holly, he wished to hell he'd never heard of Meredith Preston or hired her. Because she was messing up his life.

Chapter Seven

Too honest.

Could a man be too honest with a woman?

Cooper had tossed and turned all night. Finally he'd crossed his arms under his head and stared at the ceiling until the sun lifted itself over the horizon. Early-morning chores he'd handled all of his adult life couldn't take his mind off Meredith. As he fed the horses, he decided he'd like to take her riding sometime. *If* she was still around to ask. Maybe, in spite of his silence last night, she'd pack up her belongings and leave, anyway.

When he returned to the house, Meredith was standing at the counter, scooping coffee into the coffeemaker. She looked up at him, then she looked away. Her usual morning smile was missing as was a chipper "Good-morning."

"I need Clarice Barlow's phone number," she informed him before he could figure out what to say.

"You're still going to meet with her?"

"I told you I would."

"I thought after last night—"

"Last night you just confirmed what you've been telling me all along. Maybe now I'll believe you." Her voice was as cool as it had been last night, except for when she'd said good-night to Holly.

Suddenly Cooper felt a prick on his ankle. When he looked down, he saw the yellow tabby clawing its way up his leg. Stooping, he scooped it into his hand as Holly came down the stairs.

The kitten meowed, and he scratched it behind its ear with his thumb. It purred and then licked his finger. The little fella was still so small.

Holly rushed into the kitchen. "There you are! I opened the door to my room and he disappeared." She was holding the calico kitten and took the tabby from him, too. "I'll put them in the laundry room till I get their breakfast."

"She's taking good care of them," Cooper commented as his daughter went down the short hall.

"Yes, she is," Meredith agreed.

The long silence reminded him Meredith wasn't going to make conversation when she had nothing to say to him. And he wasn't going to apologize to her for speaking the truth or for a kiss they'd both enjoyed. "After I shave and shower, I'll get you Clarice's number."

Meredith nodded that she'd heard him, then she took a box of cereal from a cupboard. He strode to the stairs feeling as if he'd lost something, but not sure what.

When Cooper returned home from work that evening, the atmosphere between him and Meredith hadn't changed. She'd called him at the store to tell him she'd set up a meeting with Clarice and her friends at Murphy's Furniture the following afternoon. Then she'd said goodbye and hung up before he could tell her he'd bring home catalogs of his product lines so she could look over them.

Supper was quiet. Even Holly seemed subdued by the tension between them, and he knew he had to do something about it. While Meredith and Holly sat in the backyard on a blanket playing cards, with the kittens cavorting around them, he worked in his shop. After he read Holly a story and put her to bed, he retrieved the catalogs from his truck and found Meredith sitting on the back porch.

She glanced over her shoulder when he opened the screen door, then stood. Without a word she tried to pass him to go inside, but he caught her arm. "You said you'd like to become familiar with my product lines. These catalogs should help you do that. If you come into the store before your appointment, I can show you what we have in stock. I checked with Alma, and she's free to watch Holly for however long you're gone."

As Meredith pulled from his grasp and took the catalogs from him, her hand brushed his, and she quickly jerked away.

"Meredith..."

"I'll take these upstairs and go through them now."

He knew he couldn't let her go inside without mending fences between them. As she opened the door, he said, "Wait."

The glow from the light outside his shop reached the back porch. He saw the lift of her chin just before she asked, "Why?"

"Because we have to talk."

"I don't think there's anything to talk about," she replied with a sadness that hurt him.

"You're wrong." When her soft green eyes just studied him, he felt unnerved and awkward. "Dammit, Meredith, I don't know what to do about you!"

Her brows arched, and he knew he'd made a bad start. "I like you, Meredith. I like being around you. I like kissing you, and I like touching you. But I can't tell you there's ever going to be any more than that. If that's too honest for you, then you'll have to decide if you should leave.''

She gazed up at him. ''I like being around you, too, Cooper. And when you kiss me... No man's ever made me feel that way before. But I won't go to bed with you just for the thrill of it. So maybe you're the one who should decide if I should leave.''

Honesty met with honesty. Meredith didn't play coy games; she didn't try to manipulate him. Tina hadn't been honest with him about what she'd wanted from her life. When she'd told him she was leaving, she'd admitted she'd always wanted more excitement than Harmony Hollow or her marriage to him could give her. Their life together had been a stepping-stone for her. She'd destroyed his dreams to chase after hers without a backward glance.

Cooper admired Meredith's honesty, her ability to lay everything on the table and stand her ground. ''I don't want you to leave.''

''Because of Holly?''

''Yes.'' He saw the disappointment flicker in her eyes. ''But not only because of Holly. Since Tina left, I've been pretty numb. From the night you arrived, that's changed. I think you're good for me, too, Meredith. I just don't like admitting it.''

When she gave him a slow smile, he knew the strain between them had lifted. What was left was the tingling excitement that had been there since the night they'd met. Though he wanted to kiss her, he knew that could get them into trouble again. So he asked, ''Would you like to see the special order I've been working on?''

Her smile became brighter. ''Sure.'' She laid the catalogs on the lawn chair on the porch and followed him to his shop.

For the past twenty-four hours, Meredith had been trying to decide whether it would be better to stay at Cooper's...or leave. Attached to Holly and falling in love with Cooper, she'd tried to analyze what was best for all of them. But her mind and her heart had been at odds until Cooper had asked her to stay and had given her hope.

As she followed him through the space with machines to the room beyond which smelled more strongly of wood and varnish, she spotted a dark pine dining room set—a table, chairs and hutch. She crossed to the hutch and ran her hand over the cabinet door. "This is beautiful!"

"It did turn out well. I have to put a finish coat on it yet. The couple who ordered it is driving up from New York on Friday to pick it up."

Meredith tried to open the cabinet door. When it stuck, Cooper reached for the knob, and his fingers covered hers. She went still and he took her hand in his, turning her toward him.

"Tell me about your marriage," he demanded gruffly.

She didn't talk about it with anyone, but she had the feeling Cooper would understand. And for some reason tonight, unlike last night, it seemed right to confide in him. "I married Brian because I thought we were suited to each other, because we could build a good life together. We both wanted children and started trying right away. After my first miscarriage, Brian was kind...understanding. We promised each other we'd try again when we were both ready. And we did."

Pausing, she felt more vulnerable sharing what had happened next. "But after the second miscarriage, he became distant. I was afraid to become pregnant, and he wasn't there when I needed to talk or cry. He began coming home later and later, went on more business trips. I started having suspicions. I think a woman knows when—'' Thinking about it still hurt, and she couldn't be dispassionate about Brian's infidelity.

"That bastard!" Cooper's brown eyes were filled with the agony he felt for her.

"After I saw proof of his affair, I blamed myself, I blamed what had happened. But I thought we still had a chance. I hoped if we went to counseling, really communicated..." She shook her head. "He wanted no part of it. He wanted a divorce so he could marry his...his lover. A few months later I heard she was pregnant."

"Meredith, I'm sorry."

She took a deep breath. "I understand anger and betrayal. But, Cooper, I could only be happy again when I let go of the anger."

Silent for a moment he finally said, "You could cut your ties to your ex-husband. You didn't have a—'' He stopped abruptly, and she knew he didn't want to hurt her.

"You can say it. Brian and I didn't have a child to think about, to share, to love. I know you believe Holly makes your divorce more complicated, but she should also make it easier because you have proof of your love. Your marriage gave you a precious gift, Cooper."

His expression became tender as he drew Meredith toward him. "You are a beautiful, desirable woman and your ex-husband was a jerk." As if he needed to prove it to her, Cooper began to lower his lips to hers...then suddenly stopped. "This is probably not a good idea."

Although she wanted to feel his lips on hers again, wanted to feel his arms around her, wanted to feel she was beautiful and desirable to him, she agreed. "Probably not."

Straightening, he asked, "Would you like to go riding? Tomorrow evening?"

"I'd like that. Holly will want to come along."

"I'm sure she will. And I think she's ready. We can just walk the horses down to the stream."

When he brushed his thumb across Meredith's cheek-bone, every nerve in her body trembled. "I'd better go in and look through those catalogs."

"You mean you'd better go in before I kiss you."

She nodded. Cooper might be ready to admit he liked having her around, but she didn't think he was ready to trust her enough to open his heart. Maybe in time...

"I'll see you in the morning," she murmured.

"In the morning," he repeated, his brown eyes golden with unfulfilled desire.

She ran her hand over the beautiful grain of the hutch once more, wishing she could touch Cooper with the same freedom. Then, banishing the thought, she headed for the night and cooler air and the porch, her heart humming a song that was filled with hope.

Late Wednesday afternoon, Meredith was making a batch of brownies from a mix. Cooper had shown her around the store today, explaining brands and quality. After her appointment with Clarice's friends, she'd handed him an order that had raised his brows in amazement. She'd enjoyed talking with the women, expressing her opinions on color, placement of furnishings and accessories. Now both she and Holly were looking forward to riding with Cooper tonight. Holly had rested earlier while under Alma's care and was now sitting at the kitchen table working on math.

When the phone rang, Meredith stuck her wooden spoon into the brownie batter and answered it.

"Meredith, it's Tina. Have you talked to Cooper?"

Meredith glanced at Holly. "I did. But he won't budge. Maybe if you try to talk to him again…"

"He's mule-headed when he thinks he's right."

"He's trying to keep Holly safe. Maybe if you can prove to him *you* have her best interests at heart…"

"How can I do that when he won't let her visit?"

"You could do it here. If you make this a power struggle, Holly is the one who will lose."

"Is that what I'm doing? Making it a power struggle?"

"Can you truly not get away for at least a few days?"

The silence that met her question made Meredith wonder if she'd pressed too hard. But Tina had shoved her into the middle of this.

"I'll look at my schedule again," she finally replied. "Can you put Holly on?"

Meredith held out the phone to the eight-year-old. "It's your mom."

When Holly took the receiver, Meredith mixed the brownie batter vigorously. Someone had to champion Holly. And if that meant bringing Tina back to Harmony Hollow, well, it would be an eye-opener to see Cooper and Tina together. Maybe then she'd learn how he really felt about his ex-wife.

As Cooper saddled the horses, he found himself whistling. How long had it been since he whistled? Holly brought him a saddle blanket, and he threw it over Gypsy.

"Can I go to Marsha's tomorrow afternoon? Her mom said I can stay for supper if I do."

Before her accident, Holly had been an active child and a very social one. She'd loved being with her friends. But since she'd been home, she'd been hesitant to see them, because of her scars, because of her limp. He was glad she felt comfortable with Marsha. "Sure, you can. I'll clear it with Meredith."

As he straightened the saddle blanket, Holly stood by his side, chewing on the nail of one finger. He suspected there was something else on her mind. But rather than push, he swung the saddle from the top rung of the stall to Gypsy's back.

"Mommy said she's gonna buy me a new saddle. A special one—with fancy stuff on it."

Cooper felt his body tense as it always did when he thought of Tina. "Did you talk to your mom today?" He knew Holly called Tina and didn't tell him. Hoping he could make the way for his daughter to be freer with him, he tried to keep his interest casual.

"Yep." His daughter gave him a sideways glance. "She talked to Meredith for a while."

Meredith hadn't mentioned it when he'd gotten home or during supper. "Did *you* call your mom?"

"Uh-uh. She called me."

"But she wanted to talk to Meredith?"

"Meredith answered. I think Mom wanted to know if I could go see her. But Meredith said you wouldn't budge. Why won't you budge, Dad? I know you said you and Mommy won't be married anymore. Ever. But I still wanna be."

He couldn't ignore the plea in his daughter's eyes, but he had to do what he thought was right, too. Crouching down beside Holly, he wrapped his arm around her. "Your mom and I aren't married anymore and never will be. She left us, Holly, because she wants a different kind of life in a big city with a lot more to do than we have in Harmony Hollow. But even though she left, she's still your mom and I'm still your dad and that will *never* change. When you got hurt, I decided you're not old enough to spend time with her in New York.''

"When will I be old enough?"

He wanted to say "never" but knew he couldn't. "I'm not sure."

"When I'm ten?"

"When you're ten, we'll talk about it again."

Holly frowned. "I like taxi rides and stoppin' for a hot dog and all the people. Mom says it's ex-ci-ting."

"That's why she moved there. But it's an adult world, small stuff, and you're not ready for it yet. Now let's get these horses saddled or we won't be ready by the time Meredith cleans up supper."

Holly didn't ask any more questions as Cooper finished saddling the horses and led them into the paddock. When Meredith crossed the yard and approached the fence, he saw she had tied her hair back in a low ponytail. When she opened the gate, she said, "Daniel called. He wants to know if you're still helping with the spaghetti supper on Saturday. You and he are the main chefs?" Her green eyes sparkled, and he guessed she was imagining him in front of a stove.

"Daniel has a great recipe for spaghetti sauce. A few years ago when the fire company needed a fund-raiser, somebody suggested a spaghetti supper. And somehow Daniel and I got roped into supervising it. It's all volunteer. Holly went along with me last year and helped keep the bread baskets filled. In between she played with the other kids there or colored. I think they still need waitresses," he added with a grin.

Meredith laughed. "Anything for a good cause. I'd be glad to help. Tell Daniel to add my name to his list."

"Are you sure? I was just teasing."

"I'm sure. And I can help you keep an eye on Holly."

His daughter had been petting Gypsy as he and Meredith talked. Going to the spaghetti supper would be good for her. She'd see friends from school, feel the best part of Harmony Hollow—its community spirit. Then maybe she'd forget about visiting Tina in New York.

As Meredith closed the gate and came closer to him, he realized he wanted her to feel the community spirit, too. Maybe if she did, and she became involved with the people of Harmony Hollow, she'd stay past summer.

He pushed the thoughts of fall and change aside and handed Meredith the reins to her horse.

The afternoon on Thursday belonged to Meredith, and she knew exactly what she was going to do with it. After she'd learned Holly was spending the afternoon with her friend, Meredith had asked Cooper if he'd mind if she went riding. Seeing her capability with a horse on their slow but long trail ride, he'd had no objections.

Last evening they'd walked their horses over fields and along a path through tall evergreens to a stream where yellow and white wildflowers dotted the bank. Meredith gathered up a social studies text and worksheets to take along with her as well as a paperback novel she'd started. She wanted to spend some time at that spot.

Saddling the dappled gray, Silver Spark, whom she'd ridden last night, she took him into the paddock and mounted, tucking her books under her arm. As she rode, clouds covered the sun for a while and she was glad she'd worn her sweater. Easily finding the stream and the wildflowers, she dismounted and settled in a patch of reappearing sun, planning Holly's next social studies lesson while Spark grazed by the maple where she'd tethered him.

After she'd planned the next few lessons, she propped

against a tree trunk and got lost in her novel. At first she wasn't aware of the wind picking up. But suddenly a gust swept by her, chilling her. Glancing up, she saw that clouds had again covered the sun and looked blacker by the moment. As she checked her watch, she saw that she'd lost track of time. That often happened when she read. Fortunately she'd planned tacos for supper that wouldn't require much preparation time. Cooper would be home soon.

Cooper.

She smiled and gathered her books.

A few stray drops of rain fell as she rode through the trail under the trees. Hopefully, she'd get back before the clouds loosed any more.

Emerging from the trees, she took off toward the farm Blasts of wind buffeted her as she kept her hands firm on Spark's reins. When a sudden gust caught her off guard, Holly's textbook slipped from her grasp, and notes and worksheets went flying. The white sheets in the wind spooked Spark and he reared up. Unprepared, Meredith found herself dumped on the ground, the air knocked from her lungs. It took her a moment until she realized Spark had trotted off, not intending to wait for her. She called to him, but he paid her no mind. As she took a few deep breaths, rain pelted her face and the clouds opened wide.

She'd landed on her backside and it took her a few moments to make sure she wasn't hurt. She still felt out of breath but that was from the jolt of the fall. And if she didn't get on her feet and get moving, Cooper would be home before she got back.

She didn't want him to worry. If Spark had headed back to the barn…

The rain had already soaked the papers that had blown into the wind. When she stooped to pick up the textbook and the novel, she winced. Her hip hurt. But she couldn't worry about that. She started walking…fast.

It seemed like hours until she found her way back to Cooper's barn. The paddock was already muddy and as she stepped into it, she grimaced. Her feet felt lead weighted as it was. She'd only made it halfway across when Cooper came out the door. He was at her side in seconds.

"Spark threw me," she explained, suddenly feeling as if she couldn't take in enough air. "Is he…?"

"He's here. Are you all right?"

"Just feeling really stupid. I…I…" A rushing sound began in her ears, and gray dots floated in front of her eyes. The next thing she knew, Cooper had scooped her up into his arms and was carrying her to the house. A wave of dizziness made her lean her head against his shoulder. With her eyes closed, she couldn't see his expression but she could hear the fast thumping of his heart. He didn't stop until he'd taken her to the living room and laid her gently on the couch.

"I'll get the sofa all wet," she protested, the fuzziness clearing.

"Hang the sofa," he muttered, pulling off her short riding boots. "Don't move. I'll be back."

Move? When she felt like an overcooked noodle? Not likely. Closing her eyes, she realized her hair was as soaked as the rest of her and she was probably a real sight. After a short while, she started shivering.

Opening her eyes, she tried to lever herself up and heard Cooper's footsteps. A moment later he was gently pushing her back. "I called Holly's doctor. Does anything hurt?"

"Um…I'm so wet, it's hard to tell. Just my hip. Cooper, I'm fine. I just felt a little dizzy after walking so fast…''

"So soon after the fall," he finished. "Too much exertion when your body needed to rest. Are you sure nothing else hurts?"

This time he didn't stop her when she levered herself up. "Nothing else." But she couldn't stop chills from making her shiver.

"Are you nauseous? Still dizzy?"

"I don't have a concussion. I landed on my backside," she muttered wryly.

Cooper's lips twitched and he almost smiled. "The patient is the worst person to diagnose her own condition. Think you can manage a warm shower?"

"Of course I can."

"The doctor said to use acetaminophen and take it easy tonight."

Wanting him to believe she was capable of taking care of herself, she stood. But she felt a little unsteady and wobbled. Cooper caught her and slipped his arm around her waist.

Her breath hitched and it had nothing to do with the effects of her fall. This close to Cooper, unsteadiness took on new meaning. "I think I'll get that shower," she murmured.

"Are you sure you're steady enough?"

With him holding her, she wasn't sure of anything. "Let me go up on my own steam, and I'll find out."

He held on to her a few moments longer, as if he was reluctant to let her go. But then he released her and moved away a few inches.

Swallowing hard, she took a few steps and was relieved when the floor stayed stable under her feet. But when she reached the foot of the stairs, he came up behind her. "I'll go up with you. Leave the door open a crack, and then if you need help, you can call.''

''Cooper...''

He gave her a wicked grin. ''Afraid I'll peek?''

''Promise you won't?'' she asked half joking, half serious.

Raising his hand like a Boy Scout, he solemnly vowed, ''I promise I won't.''

She smiled. One thing she knew by now—Cooper was a man of his word. Climbing the steps slowly, she was aware of him behind her.

Searching in a drawer for a jogging suit that was as soft as it was comfortable, she took it to the bathroom with her.

Cooper handed her a fresh towel. ''Take your time. I'll be right here.''

Thanking him, Meredith slipped into the bathroom extremely aware of him right outside the door. Although he'd told her not to hurry, she moved as quickly as she could.

Once she'd showered, dried her hair and dressed, she opened the door wide. Cooper stood against the wall, one ankle crossed over the other. His gaze passed over her. ''How do you feel?''

''Like I'll break if I move too fast. *And* thoroughly foolish. When I dropped the book, the papers blew and spooked Spark. I should have used a saddlebag or something.''

Cooper didn't disagree, but he didn't scold, either. That surprised her.

''C'mon.'' He motioned toward the guest room. ''Let's get you settled.''

''But I have to make supper.''

Gently clasping her arm, he guided her to her bedroom.

"Rest, Meredith. Doctor's orders. I'll fix us something to eat."

"You don't have to do that…"

He took a strand of her flyaway hair between his fingers and played with the ends. "Are you one of those women who don't know how to let a man take care of them?"

She was used to servants and cooks and maids, but she'd never had a man take care of her before. Brian had relied on their staff to do that after her miscarriages. "I guess there's always a first time," she responded softly.

Opening her door, he waited until she went inside. "Will you be okay while I go down to the barn for a few minutes? I need to make sure Spark's sound."

"Cooper, I'm fine. Really." Fine, but suddenly very tired. Deciding that resting wouldn't be a bad idea, she sat on the edge of the bed.

Cooper studied her, as if he was looking for something. Then, unexpectedly, he crossed the room to her and towered over her. "You scared me. The way you looked when you came into the paddock…" He let out a breath. "I suppose it brought back memories of Holly's accident and how powerless I felt. You mean a lot—" He paused. "Holly depends on you. And so do I."

Was he becoming fond of her? Was he feeling more than desire? The way he'd taken care of her today so tenderly, so gently… She crooked her finger at him. When he leaned down, she kissed his cheek. "Thank you, Cooper."

He looked surprised. And terrifically pleased. In a different way than he'd looked after they'd kissed because of fiery desire. "You're welcome."

Lightly touching her shoulder, he said, "Lie back and rest." Then he looked down on her and smiled.

As he left the room, she settled back against a pillow and closed her eyes, remembering his smile.

The air-conditioning kept the social hall cool where citizens of Harmony Hollow were enjoying spaghetti, rolls, salad, iced tea and chocolate cake on Saturday. The kitchen was another matter. The steam swirling up from the boiling pots of water along with the sauce and at least ten bodies vying for space at one time created a humidity that curled the ends of Meredith's hair, though the camaraderie among the volunteers kept a smile on their faces most of the time.

She hadn't seen Cooper much. He'd come to the fire hall early this morning to help Daniel start the sauce simmering and had stayed throughout the day. Ever since he'd taken care of her Thursday night, something had changed between them. For the better. But, then again, maybe she was seeing something that wasn't really there. Maybe he did depend on her for Holly's sake, and that's all there was to it.

Though, he'd watched her carefully Thursday evening as he'd served them supper, asked how she felt often and suggested she turn in early. After Holly had returned home and they'd put her to bed, Meredith had gone to her room and slept soundly until morning. Besides feeling a little stiff on Friday, she'd had no further ill effects from the fall.

Still, Cooper thought she shouldn't overdo today. So she'd just chosen the last shift to serve, from six to eight. Ever since she'd arrived, she'd been busy. Holly had eaten with Marsha and was now sitting at a table drawing pictures with her.

Cooper left the kitchen to check supplies in the storage closet as Daniel sloshed spaghetti onto plates. When Meredith transferred them to a serving tray, she asked, "So where did you find the recipe for the sauce? I managed to taste a bit and it's good."

"Maybe we'll get a chance to actually sit down and eat a plate of spaghetti after we serve our last customer."

Since Meredith had started serving, Daniel had treated her like a friend. She liked him. He was more talkative than Cooper and spoke freely about his daughter, always with a smile on his face.

"Is the recipe a secret?" she teased when he didn't answer her question.

"Not a secret. Just special. It was my father's. His best friend, a firefighter, gave him the recipe."

"He made it often?"

This time Daniel's smile was faint. "Every Saturday evening. After my mom died, it was a ritual that became even more important. We just had each other, no other family. My dad was a special man. He always said he was just a factory worker, but he was so much more."

As Daniel continued to fill plates, Meredith asked, "Where's Susie?"

"She's with my mother-in-law. She's at the age where she thinks she should *wear* spaghetti rather than eat it." After a wry grin he said, "Holly looks completely recovered. Only a slight limp."

"By the end of the summer that should disappear. The scars are another matter."

Perceptively he remarked, "You're not talking about just the physical scars."

"No, I'm not. The accident divided her parents even more and—" She stopped, feeling as if she shouldn't discuss Cooper with his friend.

When Daniel cocked his head, he studied her. "Cooper's very lucky he found you to care for Holly."

She felt her cheeks flush.

"Cooper hasn't told you that yet?" he teased.

"I'm not sure how lucky Cooper considers himself," she admitted.

"He must have his head buried in the sand," Daniel muttered with a shake of his head.

"Not all the time," she murmured, remembering when he'd told her she was beautiful and desirable, remembering his kisses.

After studying her for a moment, Daniel grinned. "Okay, I won't pursue that one."

"Thank you," she replied with a smile.

When Cooper emerged from the storage area with packages of spaghetti, he stopped cold. Daniel and Meredith were standing side by side, close, talking intently. Gazing into each other's eyes, they looked totally absorbed. Cooper felt his heart lurch, and an emotion he never experienced before urged him to clench his fist. As he watched the two of them closely, Meredith blushed. After another short interchange, she smiled. Suddenly Cooper was filled with the desire to separate Daniel from Meredith, to pull Meredith to his side and keep her there.

He'd noticed men looking at her as she served at the long tables. Her jeans were just tight enough to stir up his libido, her breasts attractively noticeable under her knit shirt. Why hadn't she worn one of her cotton blouses rather than material that molded to her? Tendrils of hair had escaped her ponytail and wisped around her face. Her time in the sun with Holly had given her a golden tan, and a few freckles now dotted her nose. She was so damn beautiful! And it looked as if she was enjoying Daniel's company more than anyone else's.

Daniel might be a widower and still grieving for his wife, but he was also a red-blooded American male who knew a pretty woman when he saw one. It had been over a year since his wife had died. Maybe he was ready to find a mother for Susie, or even just—

Cooper cut off the thought. *Meredith isn't interested in a fling,* he told himself.

And maybe Daniel isn't, either, a devil on his shoulder whispered.

Cooper took the spaghetti to the stove, ripped open the boxes and dumped the pasta into the water.

Aware of every move Meredith made the rest of the evening, every word, glance or gesture in Daniel's direction, Cooper found himself getting more and more agitated. At one point Daniel sloshed spaghetti onto a plate and it splashed Meredith's arm. Daniel quickly found a towel and wiped the sauce away.

It was more than Cooper could handle. "Meredith, you'd better get that out there before it gets cold," he suggested in a brusque tone.

Her gaze collided with his. "I'm on my way."

He watched as she left the kitchen.

"What's wrong?" Daniel asked.

Stirring the pasta, he mumbled, "Nothing's wrong."

"Bull. You can't take your eyes off Meredith, and you keep scowling at me."

"You two seem pretty chummy."

"And you two snap, crackle and pop whenever you get within a foot of each other. But then you back off, and Meredith finds something else to occupy her. What gives?"

"Why are you so interested?" he asked warily, wondering if Daniel was planning on getting to know Meredith better.

"I'm interested because you deserve some happiness after the mess Tina made of your life."

Disconcerted, Cooper realized he'd never questioned Daniel's friendship or loyalty before and shouldn't start now. "It's tough living under the same roof with her and not—you know."

Daniel gave him a wicked grin. "Nope. I don't."

Before Cooper could think of a comeback, Meredith returned to the kitchen with an empty tray. "Cooper, Alma's out there. She said a huge package for Holly was delivered to her house this afternoon after we left. It's too heavy for her to lift, and she had the man put it in her garage."

"I'll go talk to her if you watch this and turn it off when the buzzer rings."

"No problem," Meredith replied as she came over to the stove.

He could smell her shampoo again. And a smudge of sauce dotted her chin. He couldn't help reaching out and wiping it with his thumb. The steam became part of the sensual cloud surrounding them.

Daniel cleared his throat.

When Meredith averted her gaze, Cooper scowled again at his friend. Daniel just shrugged. Swallowing an epithet, Cooper went to find Alma, wishing he could make Meredith smile as easily as Daniel had.

Chapter Eight

Letting herself and Holly into the house with the key Cooper had given her, Meredith said, "You get ready for bed. Your dad should only be a few minutes."

"Are you going to bring the kittens some milk?"

"I'll get it and be right up."

As Meredith went to the kitchen, she realized what a good time she'd had at the spaghetti supper, meeting more of Cooper's customers and neighbors. Holly's physical therapist had sought Meredith out and asked if she'd like to go shopping with her in Manchester on her next day off. Liking Nancy, Meredith had told her she would. When Clarice Barlow had introduced her to a few more of her friends, Meredith realized she was starting to feel as if she belonged in Harmony Hollow.

And more than once she'd felt Cooper's gaze on her.

Crossing to the refrigerator, she saw the light blinking on the answering machine. When she pressed the button, she heard Becca's voice.

"Meredith? Cooper? Luke and I would like you to

come and spend the Fourth of July with us next Sunday. You know we have plenty of room, and Holly will love my new horse. Think about it and let us know.''

Meredith would love to see Luke, Becca and her son, Todd. It had been a while. But… Could she count on Luke and Becca not to tell Cooper about her background? If he knew she was wealthy, she had the feeling he'd look at her differently, that the wall guarding him would become thicker and higher.

As she was trying to decide whether or not to call Becca, the front door opened. Going to the foyer, she saw Cooper kick the door closed with his foot while he hoisted a large box higher in his arms.

''Is Holly upstairs?'' he asked.

When Meredith nodded, he called up the stairs. ''Holly? Can you come down? Your mom sent you something.''

Holly rushed down the stairs as Cooper set the box on the living room floor. ''I wonder if it's…''

''It's heavy enough to be a saddle,'' he said with a frown. ''Let's see.''

He ripped open the carton easily, but let Holly raise the flaps. ''Oh, Daddy, look. It *is* a saddle.''

''Sure is.'' He snapped his mouth shut as if he wanted to say more but wouldn't. As he lifted it from the box, Meredith could see this was not an ordinary saddle. The tool work on the leather was extraordinary, the quality of the leather and crafting exquisite.

''Gypsy will love it. Can I call Mom and thank her?'' Holly ran her hand over the seat lovingly, a radiant smile on her face.

''Go ahead. You can call from my bedroom.''

After a last pat on the leather, Holly hurried upstairs. Cooper's gaze met Meredith's after Holly was out of earshot. "It's handmade and should probably be insured. She'll grow out of it in a year the way she's sprouting up. This is what Tina does now to make up for not being here. She thinks money and expensive presents will make Holly happy. I don't want my daughter thinking that's true."

"Holly seemed pleased."

"Oh, she's pleased for the moment. But Tina's extravagant life-style doesn't make up for Holly not having a mother to hug her, and brush her hair and put her to bed at night." He raked his hand through his hair. "Yet I'm beginning to realize if Tina had stayed and she wanted a different life than I did, that wouldn't have been good for Holly, either."

Impulsively Meredith clasped his arm. "You're doing a good job with Holly."

Cooper's expression eased. "So are you. She's much happier since you've been here."

Meredith waited, thinking he might kiss her, but instead he took her hand in his and said, "You and Daniel seemed to be getting along well."

"I like Daniel."

He frowned. "You do?"

"Cooper, what do you want to know?" she asked softly.

He looked unsettled and released her hand. "Nothing."

"I think you do. I think you want to know if I'm attracted to Daniel."

The nerve in his jaw worked. "Are you?"

"Daniel's a handsome man, but..."

"But?" Cooper asked, studying her.

"You're the man who makes my pulse race," she admitted, not sure exactly how much of a risk to take.

"And Daniel doesn't?"

"Daniel doesn't."

Cooper's head lowered slowly as he wrapped his arms around her. When his lips covered hers, her pulse raced, her heart pounded, her knees went weak, and she knew she'd fallen in love. She couldn't tell Cooper about her background yet, not until he realized her upbringing and her bank account didn't matter as much as a life with him could. As she gave herself up to his kiss, she decided she'd ask Becca and Luke to keep her secret—just for a little while—just until Cooper could admit he had feelings for her as well as desire.

During the drive to Connecticut early on the Fourth of July, Meredith kept Holly occupied with playing traveling games—like finding consecutive letters of the alphabet on license plates, naming types of trees and flowers, singing rounds of songs with Cooper joining in. Meredith had to admit she wanted to keep herself occupied, as well as Holly, because she was nervous about this trip.

When Cooper decided he liked the idea of taking Holly to Connecticut for the Fourth, Meredith had phoned Becca and asked her stepsister to keep her wealthy background a secret. Neither Luke nor Becca approved of the idea, but both had agreed to honor her request. Cooper's reaction to the saddle Tina had sent reinforced the fact that he'd look at Meredith differently if he knew she didn't need to be working at all!

Meredith understood his dismay at Tina sending presents rather than spending time with her daughter, because Meredith's father had done the same thing. After their mother died, he had showered her and Paula with gifts, thinking material possessions could soothe their loss. Instead of spending time with them, he left presents. If he missed important events in their lives, he bought them more gifts. When he remarried, he carried on the pattern, including Becca. The three of them were used to it by now.

As Cooper turned off the highway and drove along a road lined with maples and poplars, Meredith's trepidation grew. Maybe she should have made some excuse for not wanting to come.

You're only staying overnight. Calm down.

The access road leading to the property was bordered by a split rail fence. At the end of it, a decades-old stone house nestled between tall spruce. The rustic appeal of the setting reminded Meredith why she loved visiting here—besides spending time with Luke, Becca and Todd.

Cooper parked her car in front of the detached garage. She'd offered him the use of it for the trip, thinking Holly would be more comfortable with the room in the back seat in case she wanted to stretch her leg. Cooper had agreed the idea was a good one, but admitted he preferred driving. Knowing Cooper was a man who couldn't sit back and relax while someone else controlled his destiny, she'd handed him the keys, feeling safe with him—as always.

Todd came galloping down the front steps of the picturesque house. Twelve now, he seemed to grow a few more inches every time she saw him. Luke and Becca followed him at a more leisurely pace. Quickly opening her door, Meredith climbed out and hugged all three of them. Cooper shook hands amid greetings until Todd asked Holly, "Want to go to the stable?"

After Holly knew they were coming, she'd gone on and on about Todd's horse. He had let her ride the Appaloosa when she and her dad had delivered furniture after Luke and Becca moved in.

Now she looked up at Cooper expectantly. "Can I, Dad?"

Luke clapped Cooper's shoulder. "Todd knows Holly has been recuperating. They'll just feed the horses some carrots."

Without making a big deal of Holly's accident, Luke was letting Cooper know that Holly was safe with his stepson. Luke was as tall as Cooper, his brown hair a shade lighter, his build as muscular. Cooper had told her that his uncle and Luke's father had been army buddies, and he and Luke had connected on and off over the years. Since Luke had married Becca, they'd been in touch more often.

Cooper studied Todd for a few moments—his oversize T-shirt, jeans and sneakers—then he glanced at Becca and caught her almost imperceptible nod that Todd would watch over his daughter carefully.

"Okay, small stuff. Go see the horses while we settle in."

Becca warned her son, "Lunch is in half an hour."

Todd lifted a hand in acknowledgment, then led Holly to the path alongside the house that wended to the stables.

When Cooper took their suitcases from the trunk, Becca said, "I'll show you to your rooms."

"I'll get Meredith's suitcase," Luke offered, then caught Meredith's elbow as Cooper and Becca went into the house. "Do you know what you're doing?" he asked her.

He didn't have to explain what he meant.

"No more than you did."

"My point exactly," he returned grimly.

Luke had met and fallen in love with Becca under false pretenses. CEO of the foundation his family had created, at least once a year he traded his suit for jeans and a hard hat and supervised a project. Becca had been awarded a small business grant, and Luke had acted as general contractor on her restaurant in Pennsylvania. During those weeks he worked outside of his office, he pretended to be an ordinary guy, rather than a man born of wealth. As Luke had become more involved with Becca, Meredith and Paula had decided to protect their stepsister by checking into his background, and discovered he was much more than he seemed.

"You know how betrayed Becca felt when she found out about my life here. I almost lost her," Luke added with a warning lift of his brows.

"My situation is different. You had a whole other life you had to return to. But I don't. I could make Cooper and Holly my world without looking back. My bank account has nothing to do with what I'm doing in Harmony Hollow or the future."

"Then why can't you tell Cooper about it?" Luke asked.

"Because he's already wary of Tina and her new lifestyle. If he knew I was used to luxury cars and limousines and designer clothes, he'd automatically assume all that means as much to me as it does to her. I want him to really know me first…to realize I could be happy in Harmony Hollow with him and Holly."

This past week had been lovely. She'd felt as if she was really part of a family. Although Cooper hadn't kissed her since after the spaghetti supper, he wasn't shying away from her or putting distance between them. He seemed to be getting used to the idea that he liked her in his life.

"You love him?" Luke asked gently.

"I know it seems like it happened awfully fast…"

"Not when I remember the first time I saw Becca," he

responded with a smile that said he could still picture it vividly.

"So...you'll be discreet?" Meredith pressed.

He picked up her suitcase. "I'll be the model of discretion. For now. But if you don't want this to blow up in your face, you should tell Cooper the truth. And soon."

Since Luke had married Becca, he'd become the big brother she'd never had. "I will. I just need a little more time. And Cooper needs more time."

Draping his free arm around her shoulders, Luke guided her up the steps. "Becca and I will make sure the two of you have some time alone."

Meredith gave him a grateful smile and another hug, realizing not for the first time that Becca had married a very special man.

After lunch, Becca suggested Cooper and Meredith go riding while she and Luke played croquet with Holly and Todd. Cooper saw the disappointed look on his daughter's face. "When Meredith and I get back, I'll take you out for a while. Deal?"

Holly smiled. "Deal."

"Would you like to go riding?" he asked Meredith, holding her gaze with his. He'd tried to play it casual with her this past week for both their sakes. But trying to keep the fire between them tamped down was tough.

Pushing her chair away from the table, she smiled. "I'll go get my boots."

A short while later, Meredith helped Cooper saddle two horses. When she handed him the second saddle blanket, their fingers brushed. The heat that swept through Cooper urged him to scoop Meredith onto his horse with him and ride to someplace very private. Instead, he hoisted the saddle onto the blanket.

Since Cooper had only ridden here with Luke a few times, he let Meredith choose a trail. As they gave their horses their heads across a field, he wondered where she'd learned to ride and when. In spite of her tumble, from the first time he'd seen her on Spark he'd known she was an experienced rider. The thought blew out of his head with the July breeze as they seemed to ride in unison, enjoying the feel of freedom, enjoying the day, enjoying being together. It was an odd feeling for him to enjoy the company of a woman again.

Eventually they slowed their horses to a trot, then walked them through stands of pines back to the stable. Cooper dismounted and opened the gate, then walked through and waited for Meredith to ride into the paddock. After he closed the gate, he walked up to her and held her horse while she dismounted. Her hair was disheveled from the ride, a few strands wisping out of place along her cheek. Her green eyes sparkled with her spirit and her enjoyment of the ride. But there was something else, too.

The toes of his boots barely touched hers; the lights in her eyes bent his head to hers. His lips pressed in a chaste kiss until his tongue coaxed hers apart. When her arms slid around his back, he cradled her face in his hands, then angled her mouth under his, greedily taking, possessing, needing her to assuage his desire and banish the loneliness that seemed to have been with him forever. Even his marriage to Tina hadn't eased it, though he'd expected it to.

But he forgot about the loneliness whenever he was near Meredith. And when he kissed her...

His arms tightened around her, and the loneliness disappeared.

"Dad, I'm ready! Todd said I could use—"

Holly's voice caught at the sight of him and Meredith

in an embrace, and he raised his head, abruptly dropping his arms. His daughter's brown eyes were huge, her mouth slightly rounded.

"Holly…" he began.

"You used to kiss Mommy like that!"

His first thought was that he'd *never* kissed Tina like that. Not so soul-wrenchingly needy. But when Holly spun around and headed into the stable, he ignored the underlying emotion and went after her.

Meredith caught his arm. "What are you going to tell her?"

Swearing, he muttered, "I have no idea," pulled away and strode into the stable. He found his daughter stroking the nose of Becca's new bay mare. Approaching her, he laid his hand on her shoulder.

Holly kept her gaze averted and continued to stroke the horse's nose. "Do you ever still kiss Mommy?" she asked.

Cooper kept his voice even. "No. Not since before our divorce."

"Why were you kissing Meredith?"

Seeking the simplest explanation for his daughter to understand, he answered, "Meredith and I are friends."

His daughter faced him. "You and Mrs. Macavee are friends but you don't kiss her."

Sometimes he forgot how logical Holly could be and how perceptive. "Meredith and I have a special friendship."

"The kind of friendship you had with Mommy when you were married?"

Blowing out a breath, he decided it was too difficult to explain explosive chemistry to a child. "Sort of."

"You and Mommy aren't ever going to be married again," she said as if she actually believed it now.

"No, we're not."

When he heard light footsteps, he glanced toward the door. Meredith came toward them, her expression concerned. "Holly, are you okay?"

The eight-year-old nodded slowly, and Cooper suspected she was thinking about what she'd seen.

Meredith dropped down on one knee in front of her and asked, "Are you upset about me and your dad kissing?"

Cooper winced at her forthrightness, but he admired it and knew he should have asked that question.

Holly hesitated. "I...don't know. Dad said you're friends. Special friends. Not like him and Mrs. Macavee."

Meredith's green gaze lifted to his for a moment. "No, not like him and Mrs. Macavee." Returning her attention to Holly, she asked, "You know I'm *your* friend, don't you?"

Holly nodded. "I know."

"How do you feel about your dad and I being special friends?" Meredith asked.

Holly looked from Meredith to Cooper, then back at Meredith. "I guess it's okay if you kiss Dad since he doesn't kiss Mommy anymore."

Cooper watched Meredith's cheeks flush. To try to get them all off the hook, he asked Holly, "Are you ready to go riding now?"

Nodding, she pointed to the tack room. "Todd said I can use his saddle if you want to switch them."

Meredith rose to her feet. "I'll go see if Becca needs help with supper. Have a good ride."

Holly gave her a shy smile. "We will."

As Meredith left the stable, Cooper took his daughter's hand and they headed for the tack room. He was determined to assure Holly that she was the center of his universe and that fact wouldn't change whether he kissed Meredith or not.

Red, white and blue flares exploded against the black night as Meredith sat between Cooper and Holly on a bale of hay in the loft of the stable. Luke had opened wide the short double doors so they could watch the fireworks display from a bird's-eye view.

But Meredith's thoughts were occupied with more than Roman candles and bursts of light. She and Cooper hadn't had another private moment since Holly had caught them kissing. Apparently he'd explained the intimacy to Holly by saying he and Meredith were "friends." During the picnic that had followed and games of lawn darts, Meredith wondered if she'd deluded herself into thinking they were more than friends. Maybe to Cooper a kiss *was* just a kiss, and desire *was* simply desire. Maybe he *could* keep his emotions separate from his physical needs.

When Holly had first turned away and bolted, Meredith had been afraid the little girl couldn't accept another woman with her father. But their brief conversation and her unaltered attitude toward Meredith since indicated she felt close to her and didn't see her as a threat.

As white bursts of light formed a parachute shape, Holly nudged Meredith's arm. "Can you come to bed when I do?"

Becca had put Meredith and Holly in a guest room with twin beds, beds that Cooper had crafted. They were as beautiful as the dining room set he'd also designed for Luke and Becca. But the guest room was large and the house somewhat strange to Holly, though she'd stayed once before.

Filled with affection for this child she'd come to love, Meredith replied, "I can come to bed with you. I know you'll miss having Muffin and Daisy with you.'' Holly had named the kittens herself, and at her urging they'd called Alma earlier to make sure she'd remembered to feed them.

Cooper's shoulder brushed Meredith's as he shifted toward her. ''If you want to stay up and talk with Luke and Becca, I can sit with Holly till you come up.''

All evening Meredith had tried to keep some space between her and Cooper, but with six of them in the confines of the hayloft, that was difficult. She'd been *very* aware of Cooper on the bale beside her for the past twenty minutes. ''It's been a long day. I'll be ready to turn in.''

Only the moon shed its glow into the loft until a final giant barrage of fireworks claimed the sky. Meredith could tell Cooper's gaze was on her, but she stared straight ahead and kept perfectly still. He didn't shift away.

After the last flares of light had disappeared, Luke switched on his flashlight and climbed down the ladder first so he could help Becca and then Todd and Holly. Carefully, Meredith descended the ladder followed by Cooper.

As the others headed for the door and the path to the house, Cooper said, ''Meredith, wait.''

She stopped, and he called to Luke, ''We'll get the light in here.''

A yellow bulb glowed in the storage area of the barn. Gazing up at Cooper, Meredith waited.

''You've been quiet tonight.''

''I've been thinking.''

''About Holly?''

''And about us.''

After a full three heartbeats, he confessed, ''Dammit, Meredith, I didn't know what to tell her. How can I explain what's between us to a child when I have trouble explaining it to myself?"

She realized the insecurity she'd felt after her divorce, the sense that she wasn't good enough, or whole enough, or attractive enough to keep her husband still plagued her. That's why she believed Cooper could easily dismiss whatever he felt for her.

With a gentle touch to her shoulder, he brought her closer. "I know we're more than friends. But beyond that, I'm not willing to label it." He lifted her chin with his thumb. "Holly gave her permission for me to kiss you. Since we have some privacy, maybe we should take advantage of it."

It sounded as if Cooper was willing to explore his feelings now, rather than deny them. It sounded as if there was hope. "You have my permission, too," she murmured as the scent of hay and summer and Cooper wound around her.

When he lowered his head and kissed her, the fireworks started all over again.

After Cooper opened the trunk of Meredith's car the next morning, he lifted the suitcases inside. Feeling relaxed, content, peaceful...had become a foreign concept to him. Yet this morning, he realized he felt all three. This visit with Luke and Becca had been good for him and Holly. Last night in the barn, he'd kissed Meredith until his hands had shaken, his body had throbbed and his good sense had exploded like one of those Roman candles. When she'd finally pulled away, he'd swallowed his protest, knowing exactly where she stood on taking the kiss to the empty stall a few feet away.

The anticipation was killing him. But the hope that there would soon be more than anticipation had led him to curve his arm around her waist and walk her back to the house without pushing her, simply enjoying the excitement of unfulfilled desire. Maybe when they returned home...

He smiled.

After a breakfast that should keep his appetite for food, at least, satisfied for the rest of the day, Holly had said goodbye to the horses. Now she and Todd were playing a final round of croquet. Todd was growing into a fine young man and had acted as a protective big brother to Holly throughout the visit. He called Luke "Dad," and Cooper could see how proud Luke was of his stepson.

Cooper packed the car and went back into the house. Hearing Meredith and Becca's voices in the kitchen, he crossed the foyer and stopped when he heard Becca ask Meredith, "Are you doing anything special for your birthday on Friday?"

"No. In fact, I have an appointment with one of Cooper's customers in the evening to discuss furnishing her new family room."

"Are you really enjoying helping these women furnish and decorate their homes?"

"I really am! It's fun. I have an appointment on Wednesday, too."

"You're even getting paid for your time," Becca said with amusement in her tone.

"I know. I thought about refusing payment, but that would seem unusual. It feels good earning it. Just like receiving my salary at the end of the week for taking care of Holly feels good. Maybe I'll put that into a special account."

Why would Meredith even think about refusing payment? Because she thought she didn't deserve it? She didn't realize just how talented she was, not only in giving decorating advice but in handling people. Though why she'd need a special account, he didn't understand. Maybe she was trying to live frugally while she was in Harmony Hollow in order to save for something.

Not wanting the women to think he was eavesdropping, he continued across the dining room, his footfalls sounding on the hardwood floor. When he reached the kitchen doorway, Meredith looked up and her face flushed.

He smiled, wondering if she was remembering last night's kiss or thinking about returning home and having the privacy to explore their passion further. "Ready?" he asked.

Hopping off the bar stool, she replied, "Whenever you are."

When he held out his hand to her, she took it, and he couldn't wait to get home.

About five miles from Harmony Hollow, Meredith glanced over her shoulder at Holly who'd fallen asleep. "Holly. We're almost home," she said softly.

The eight-year-old's eyes fluttered open, and she gave Meredith a sleepy smile.

"Did you have a good time?" Cooper asked Meredith with a quick look at her.

"I had a great time," she replied with a smile.

Meredith had been taken aback when Cooper walked into Becca's kitchen this morning while they were talking. But since he hadn't questioned her or commented on the conversation, she'd assumed he hadn't overheard. She didn't want him finding out about her background by accident. Luke was right. The situation could blow up in her face. As soon as they had some time alone, she'd tell him everything.

When Cooper turned onto the road leading to his house,

Meredith felt as if she were coming home, too. She'd found a sense of belonging with Cooper and Holly that she couldn't *ever* remember experiencing. After her mother died, a sense of home seemed to have vanished. Her father's remarriage certainly hadn't provided it. Their stepmother had been a practical rather than warm person with an eye on social climbing. The house where she'd lived with Brian had been mostly for show, befitting their position in the community. And her condo was elegant and comfortable but...

A home needed people who cared about one another. A home wrapped love around you every time you walked into it.

As Cooper drove down the road that was now familiar to Meredith, Holly exclaimed, "There's a car in the driveway!"

There *was* a car in the driveway—a luxury sedan.

Cooper frowned. "I don't know who could be waiting for us." As he pulled onto the gravel, he saw the car was empty but the front door of the house was open!

"Only one person has a key besides Alma," he said in a taut tone.

"Mom?" Holly asked eagerly.

"Let's go find out." He unfastened his seat belt with a snap and threw open his door.

They could hear the music blaring through the screen door as soon as they neared the house. Meredith recognized the score from a Broadway show.

Cooper crossed the threshold first, then Holly, then Meredith. By the time Meredith realized the music was blasting from a portable CD player sitting on the coffee table, Holly had run to her mother who was playing with Daisy and Muffin on the floor by the fireplace. Holly scrambled down beside Tina, and her mother gave her a huge hug.

Meredith had seen a picture of Tina in Holly's bedroom. She was a petite woman with brown hair a redder shade than Holly's. The cut was short and blunt, tapered in the back, shaped longer by her cheeks. It definitely had the style of a New York salon cut. Her makeup was expertly applied, daytime chic.

When Cooper switched off the CD player, Tina gave Holly a kiss on the cheek and stood, looking as defensive as her ex-husband. "I wanted to surprise Holly and never expected you to be away. When I arrived late last night, I slept in her room. This morning Alma told me you'd be back today."

"It's a surprise, all right," he muttered, then motioned to the proliferation of bags on the sofa. "What's all this?"

"I brought Holly a few things. And the CD player. I thought it was about time she became familiar with some show music, and some classical pieces I thought she'd like."

Cooper picked up a few of the disc cases on the table then set them down again. "She's only eight."

"It's never too soon to introduce children to good music. Ask her teacher." With an uncertain smile, Tina crossed to Meredith and offered her hand. "I've been looking forward to meeting you."

Translated, Meredith knew that meant Tina had been curious about what she looked like and probably countless other things. Meredith took note of Cooper's discomfort as she shook Tina's hand. "Holly talks about you often," Meredith said truthfully.

"I suppose you're planning to continue to stay here?" Cooper asked, his voice even.

"I'd like to." Tina sounded unsure. "I'm only staying till Thursday morning. I have to be in L.A. by Friday."

Holly hurried over to Cooper. "I want her to stay here, Dad. She has to. It'll be almost like—"

When Holly stopped, Meredith knew she had to offer a solution to the awkwardness. "Why don't I stay at a motel until—"

"No!" Cooper said sharply, looking as if he'd surprised himself. Raking his hand through his hair, he added, "It's not that long. We're not going to put Meredith out. I can bunk on the sofa. Tina, you can have my room. Is everyone in agreement?"

Tina shrugged. "It's fine with me. As long as I get some time alone with Holly."

Cooper dug one hand into his jeans pocket. "Fine. Just so you don't drive her anywhere."

Meredith caught the hurt look that crossed Tina's face. But she gave in to his condition quickly. "We'll let you drive us when we want to go somewhere. I brought enough stuff to keep us occupied right here. Holly, how would you like to go upstairs and try on your new clothes?"

"Cool!" Holly grinned and scooped up Daisy then Muffin. "Let's go."

Tina snatched up as many bags as she could and mounted the steps behind her daughter.

After Cooper watched with a look of exasperation, he turned to Meredith. "Just what I always wanted. A house party. I'll bring in the suitcases, then I'm going to the store. I'll see you at supper."

Before he took two steps, Meredith asked, "I suppose *I'm* supposed to make supper?"

His cheeks flushed. "Geez, Meredith. I'm sorry about all this. Look, if you really want to go to a motel—"

"Why do you want me to stay?"

He grimaced as if he didn't want to have this discussion any more than he liked having his ex-wife in the house. "I'm being selfish. The truth is I want you here because... Well, I don't want Tina cooking meals, *if* she remembers how, or acting as if she belongs here. That's not any better for Holly than it is for me. Things have changed. I want Tina to know that."

"So I'm some kind of statement?" Meredith asked, trying to find out if the change in Cooper's life now included her.

His expression turned stony. "You're Holly's teacher and you're my...my housekeeper. You belong here as much as Tina."

With that pronouncement he turned and opened the door.

His *housekeeper?*

Meredith blinked away hot tears and headed for the kitchen to find something in the freezer to defrost for supper.

If Cooper knew what was good for him, he'd plop the suitcases in the foyer and leave. Because if he came anywhere near her right now, she might throw something frozen at him and aim low!

Somewhere the house creaked in the middle of the night silence. Cooper punched his pillow for at least the tenth time, then sank back onto it staring at the ceiling. Moonlight illuminated the plaster as a night breeze blew through the window at the foot of the sofa.

He'd never had a problem with insomnia until Meredith arrived.

With an oath of frustration, he sat up, switched on the

table light and checked the mantel clock. It read 3:00 a.m. He stared at the steps.

His ex-wife, his daughter, his...

He swore again. His *housekeeper*. As soon as the word was out of his mouth, he'd known he'd stuck his foot in it. Meredith had been cool to him all evening and cautious with Tina. On the other hand, Holly was overjoyed her mother was here, and Tina seemed willing to make friends with Meredith.

He felt as if he didn't know which way was up. He was still so angry with Tina.

And Meredith...

He remembered her profile in the hayloft as fireworks had exploded, the softness of her lips as she'd kissed him in the barn, the sweet smell of her, her tender care of his daughter. Meredith returned his passion with hers, she was honest to a fault, she aroused him until satisfying his hunger for her became more vital than breathing.

Nope, he didn't know which way was up but he'd better find out fast or *he'd* be the one staying in a motel.

Chapter Nine

When Meredith stepped into Cooper's office at Murphy's Furniture on Wednesday afternoon, he pushed the invoices he'd been studying to one side. She laid a sales order on the desk blotter in front of him.

Before he picked it up, he suspected it would be hefty because of the look of success on her face. After he studied it, he asked, "You actually sold that abstract in the family room grouping?" That particular painting had been hanging for the past eighteen months. A customer had ordered it, then decided he didn't like it.

"The colors accented the fabric on the love seat. You really need to order a bigger selection of wall decor items."

"Do I?" he asked with a smile, knowing it was the first one that had twitched his lips since he'd found Tina in his house Monday afternoon.

"If you intend to sell total room groupings rather than merely furniture, you do."

Suddenly he wanted to make Meredith smile at

him…for him. "Maybe you could make a few selections for me from the catalogs."

"If you'd like."

"Meredith…"

"What time did Tina say she'd return to the store?"

Apparently Meredith wasn't accepting olive branches any more than Tina would return from shopping with Holly on time. Somehow he'd managed to stay civil and friendly to his ex-wife all day yesterday, even when he'd come home and found Holly's hair up in curlers and nail polish on her fingernails. This morning Tina had asked if he'd drop her and Holly at the mall on the edge of Harmony Hollow. She'd said they could walk to the store after they'd grabbed lunch and finished shopping. Cooper had made Holly promise to call him if she was too tired.

"Tina said they'd be here about one-thirty," he answered.

"Do you want me to stick around so I can drive them home?"

Meredith had driven in for her noon appointment. "You don't have to wait. I know you have better things to do."

"I can look through the wall decorations while I'm waiting if you really want me to."

"Do you know what I really want?" he asked, rising from his swivel chair and rounding the desk.

Though she asked, "What?" she took a step back.

But he still moved forward till he was close enough to touch her. "I want time alone with you, I want to kiss you, I…want to apologize for calling you my housekeeper. The world just tilted a bit when Tina arrived and I—" He stopped, not sure he could put it into words.

Wariness left her green eyes, replaced by a gentle understanding. "You're glad Holly can spend time with her mother, but you really don't want to deal with Tina yourself.''

As perceptive as always, Meredith had read his turmoil exactly right. "How did you get to know me so well?"

"Living with a person will do that," she offered softly.

He swept the curve of her hair with the backs of his fingers, just lightly touching, relishing the silkiness. "Living with a person can do a lot more." When his thumb traced her cheekbone and stopped at the corner of her lip, he felt her tremble.

"Cooper..." she murmured.

He would have closed the office door and lowered the shade right then, except he heard Holly's voice.

"Dad! Dad, look what I had done."

His daughter was hurrying toward him, brushing her hair behind her ear. At first he didn't understand what she was trying to show him. And then he saw the gold ball in her ear and realization set in. Tina had gotten his daughter's ears pierced!

All of a sudden, every change Tina had made in his daughter's appearance leaped out at him—the curled hair, the bright pink nail polish, the new clothes. "What in the hell did you do?" he asked his wife in a low tone filled with angry vehemence.

Holly's wide grin vanished, then her lower lip quivered.

Catching himself before he laid into Tina, he said, "Meredith, please take Holly home. I need to talk to her mother."

When they were married, Tina might have acceded to his wishes. But now she came forward, brown eyes flashing. "If you need to say something to me, you can say it right now. I didn't do anything wrong."

The anger wouldn't stay capped. "You mutilated my daughter!"

Holly tugged on his arm, her eyes filled with tears. "Daddy, I *wanted* to have my ears pierced. I knew you wouldn't let me, but Mommy said it was okay."

Cooper had never wanted Holly to find herself smack-dab in the middle of his anger for his ex-wife, and that's exactly what had happened. Crouching down to his daughter, he assured her, "I'm not angry with you, honey."

"No, but you're mad at Mommy. You're *always* mad at Mommy."

What had Meredith said? That if he didn't let go of the anger, Holly would resent it? Resent him? Glancing over at Meredith now, he saw that she hurt for him...for all of them.

But he didn't know *how* to let go. Taking Holly's face between his hands, he brushed away a tear. "You really wanted to have your ears pierced?"

When she nodded, he gave her a hug. Then he stood and gazed at Tina. "Why don't you and Holly go home with Meredith? I'll try to get out of here early and we can talk then."

After a glance at Cooper and then at Meredith, Tina held out her hand to her daughter. "Come on. Let's go wait outside."

Two of Cooper's employees who had overheard his outburst also headed to other parts of the store. But Meredith stayed exactly where she was and, from her expression, he knew she had something to say. "What?" he asked.

She came a few steps closer so her voice didn't carry. "You're not angry at Tina about the earrings, or even about Holly's accident. You know accidents happen, and Tina would *never* intentionally do anything to hurt Holly. Even I know that just seeing them together the past two days. You're angry at Tina because she wanted a different life from yours...because she left. Well, nothing's going to change that, Cooper, and if you don't make peace with it, with her, Holly will be torn between the two of you and have to choose a side. You'd better decide if that's what you want."

Her words carried enough truth to make him feel raw and defensive. "They're waiting for you, Meredith. And I have work to do."

"You can hide behind work if you want, and you can push me away. But that won't solve your problem. Only some good, long soul-searching might do that."

Before he could put together an adequate response, she went behind the cashier's desk and retrieved her purse, then left the store.

For the rest of the afternoon, Meredith worried whether or not she'd said too much to Cooper. Yet she knew for them to have a chance, he had to settle his differences with Tina and put their marriage finally to rest. After being around Tina and Cooper, Meredith realized they wanted very different things and maybe always had. If there had once been love between them, it was gone, and Meredith didn't think she was deluding herself about that. Cooper's resentment of Tina stemmed from the kick she'd given his ego, the pain of being abandoned. Meredith recognized it because she understood it. Brian's affair and his desire for a divorce had done the same thing to her. But she didn't hate Brian anymore; she didn't resent him. She'd put their marriage in the past. Changing the rest of her life had helped her change her emotions. In Cooper's situation, Holly reminded him of everything he'd lost.

When Cooper came home earlier than usual, the lines around his eyes were deep. He asked Tina to take a walk with him, and when his gaze met Meredith's, he looked more…peaceful than she'd ever seen him look.

Holly came over to her at the counter and asked, "Do you think he's going to yell at Mom for letting me get my ears pierced?"

Putting her arm around Cooper's daughter, she answered, "No, I don't think he is. I think everything's going to be all right."

Tina and Cooper returned about an hour later. Neither looked ruffled, in fact, they appeared more friendly. Cooper crooked his finger at Holly. Sitting on a kitchen chair, he asked, "Do you want to visit your Mom in New York?"

She nodded solemnly.

Exchanging a look with Tina, he replied, "All right. How about a week at the end of August? Your mom said she'll have you in bed at your usual time unless she has a very good reason, and she'll make sure you do kid stuff, not adult stuff."

Holly threw her arms around Cooper's neck and hugged hard. "Thank you, Daddy. Thank you, thank you."

Cooper cleared his throat, and when Holly pulled away, he added, "I'm going to try not to be angry with your mom anymore. I want you to be happy…and I want her to be happy, too. Just because we're not married now doesn't mean we can't be friendly."

Tina held out her hand to Holly. "Why don't you come upstairs and help me pack? Then tonight we can just have fun and talk about what you want to do when you come to New York."

As Tina led Holly from the kitchen, Cooper stood and approached Meredith at the sink where she'd been preparing a salad. "You were right."

"Cooper, I don't care if I was right. I just want to see you stay close to Holly."

"I know," he said, his voice dropping low. "And that's what makes you so special. Do you know how glad I am you came into our lives?"

Her heart soared with his words.

Gazing squarely into her eyes, his voice grew deeper with emotion as he said, "I *did* spend the afternoon soul-searching, and I didn't like what I saw. I don't want to be a bitter man for the rest of my life. I finally realized I've been using the accident to heap more blame on Tina and to keep Holly away from her." He took a deep breath. "I told Tina I forgive her for the accident and I want to move past it."

Meredith had sensed Cooper's strength of character from their first meeting. At this moment she loved him so much she could hardly contain the words. But she knew that she had to. He'd experienced enough emotional upheaval for one day. When she finally said *I love you* she wanted to be sure he was ready to hear it.

"You've been hurt. Badly. It's natural to want to strike out."

"I don't want to strike out anymore. I can think of much better things to do." Wrapping his arms around her, he drew her close.

She raised her lips to his for his kiss, hoping now he could learn to love again. Hoping now he could love *her*.

As Tina backed out of his driveway early Thursday morning, Cooper lifted his hand in a wave. Holly waved, too, looking a bit sad.

"You'll see your mom again in a few weeks," he reminded her.

"I know," she answered softly, her gaze following the car down the road.

Out of the corner of his eye Cooper caught the sight of Meredith in the living room. She had let them say their goodbyes to Tina alone. He had seen Tina catch Meredith's arm and heard her say thank-you before she'd come outside....

He owed Meredith a lot more than thanks. She'd become so important to him. Somehow he had to show her how important.

Out of the blue he remembered Becca asking Meredith, "Are you doing anything special for your birthday on Friday?" She deserved to celebrate her birthday in a better way than meeting with one of the customers at his store. Suddenly he decided he could use her appointment to his benefit. He was going to give her a party.

Ruffling Holly's hair, he asked her, "How would you like to help me plan a surprise party for Meredith? Her birthday's tomorrow, and I think we should celebrate."

Holly's face brightened and her eyes sparkled. "With balloons and a cake?"

He laughed. "Yep. And some people, too. We can ask Mrs. Macavee."

"And Miss Nancy," Holly added.

"And Daniel and Susie. Maybe even Mrs. Barlow." Meredith seemed to enjoy talking with her. "But you have to try to keep this a secret. Think you can do that?"

"Sure I can. We have to buy her presents," Holly reminded him.

"I'll tell her we're going to spend some time together tonight. We'll go to the mall, then stop at Daniel's and call everyone we want to invite. Sound good?"

Holly was already on her way to the door. "I'll count the money in my piggy bank."

Cooper had to smile. He wasn't sure Holly could keep a secret even until tomorrow. But she'd have fun trying.

Maybe with this party he could show Meredith what she meant to him…and figure it out himself.

The sound of the doorbell Friday afternoon interrupted Meredith's concentration as she graded Holly's morning papers and coaxed her into writing a story about Daisy and Muffin. Holly had been antsy all morning, and Meredith had decided the story would keep her student's attention focused.

Pushing her chair back, she said, "I'll get that. You keep working."

As Meredith headed for the foyer, she thought about the birthday cards she'd received in the morning mail. One from Luke, Becca and Todd, and another from her sister Paula. Maybe she should have told Cooper today was her birthday. Maybe they could have gone out for a late dinner together….

The truth was Cooper had seemed different since Tina had left. He'd seemed preoccupied. She'd understood his desire to spend last night alone with Holly, especially after Tina's visit, but he hadn't kissed her again, and she wished she could read his mind. In a few weeks the summer would be over, and if he didn't ask her to stay, she'd know his feelings had never caught up with his desire.

The delivery man at the door smiled at her. "I have a package for Meredith Preston."

"That's me," she answered with a return smile.

He handed her a small package and then asked her to sign for it. After she did, he wished her a good day and jogged to his truck.

The return address on the label caught Meredith's attention immediately. It was from her father. He'd remembered her birthday! Feeling as excited as a girl half her age, she opened the box. Inside she found another box—a velvet-covered one. When she opened it, tears came to her eyes. It was a diamond and gold brooch in the shape of a butterfly, and absolutely stunning.

At one time she'd worn jewelry like this every day. Her father hadn't understood her need to change her priorities and get her teaching degree. Just as he'd never understood that she'd rather spend an evening with him or receive a hug rather than a present. But this was his way of showing his love—she'd accepted that a long time ago.

She wished she could wear the brooch right now. She wished...

The time had come to tell Cooper everything about herself as well as her feelings for him. Maybe then he could admit what he felt for her.

Tonight.

She would tell him tonight after Holly went to bed.

Pink, white and blue helium-filled balloons bobbed in a corner of the living room where Cooper had stacked Meredith's presents. All of the guests he'd invited had arrived and now mingled in the living room while they waited for the guest of honor. Holly could hardly sit still and, at the moment, was explaining to Alma what she'd bought Meredith for her birthday.

When the telephone rang, Cooper called above the voices, "I'll get it in the kitchen."

Passing the table with the sheet cake that was decorated with flowers and candles, he smiled and picked up the phone.

"May I speak to Meredith Preston?" It was a man's voice, deep and resonating.

"She's not here right now. Can I take a message?" Cooper asked, curious about the caller.

"This is Phillip Preston. Meredith's father. I just wanted to wish her a happy birthday. I won't be able to call again this evening. I have an emergency board meeting in a few minutes."

Meredith hadn't spoken much about her father. "I'm sure she'll be upset she missed you. We're giving a surprise party for her tonight."

"You're Cooper Murphy?"

"Yes, I am. Meredith is teaching and caring for my daughter."

"So she told me. I can't understand why she wants to work as a nanny. I suppose for the same reason she insisted on volunteering in the pediatrics ward all those years when she could have been hostessing bridge clubs instead. Well, she's too old for me to interfere in her life now. Tell me, did she like the present I sent?"

"I don't know. She didn't mention receiving it," Cooper answered, his gut churning with a suspicion he didn't want to recognize.

"That's odd. Meredith loves jewelry. I would have thought she couldn't wait to wear a new diamond brooch."

A diamond brooch. Hostessing bridge clubs. A father who attended board meetings. Meredith knew fine furnishings. He should have wondered how. Needing more information, needing confirmation for his suspicions, he responded, "There aren't too many occasions to wear a diamond brooch in Harmony Hollow."

Phillip Preston chuckled. "My daughter has always been comfortable wearing jewels either at country club dinners or tennis matches."

"Meredith *is* the type of woman who deserves fine

things,'' Cooper murmured. Why hadn't he seen the signs sooner? A sense of betrayal so strong he could taste it urged him to get his bearings before Meredith arrived.

Bearings.

How could he figure out what was the truth and what were lies? He'd thought Meredith was the most honest woman he'd ever met!

''I'll tell Meredith you called,'' he said to Phillip Preston to end their conversation. He'd tell her when he confronted her about her reasons for coming to Harmony Hollow, her reasons for making a fool of him.

Preston thanked him, and Cooper hung up the phone feeling shell-shocked. Then anger took hold. He'd let go of his anger for Tina because it was past time, because she hadn't intentionally set out to hurt him or Holly. Her goals and dreams had changed, and there was no way they were compatible with his. But Meredith had hidden the truth from him for weeks! Intentionally. She'd played with his dreams and encouraged his daughter to become attached to her. For what purpose?

Why had she ever left her *real* life?

When Meredith drove down the road past Alma's house, she spotted several cars in her neighbor's driveway and wondered if Alma's relatives were visiting. Parking in front of Cooper's garage, Meredith switched off the engine and picked up her purse, her heart beating faster. Soon she'd tell Cooper she wasn't simply a teacher. Soon she'd find out if he could accept who she really was as well as her bank account.

When Meredith saw the closed front door, she assumed Holly and Cooper were out back. Using her key, she unlocked the door and pushed it open.

''Surprise!'' and ''Happy Birthday!'' came from at

least five spots in the living room. Meredith stepped back and caught her breath. Daniel, Susie, Alma, Clarice, Nancy, Holly and Cooper waited for her to say something.

"I can't believe you did this!" Her gaze found Cooper's and her heart tripped. He wasn't smiling. In fact—

Holly rushed to her side and took her hand. "Come open your presents. All this was Dad's idea. But *I* helped."

Leaving her purse on the foyer table, she let Holly lead her to the sofa. Meredith sat beside Cooper. "How did you know?"

"I overheard you and Becca talking." His tone was so serious that she wanted to ask him what was wrong but couldn't with everyone looking on.

Holly brought over a present from the corner and set it on the coffee table. "Open this one first. It's mine."

When Meredith moved forward, her arm brushed Cooper's. He quickly shifted, and again she had the feeling something was definitely wrong.

After tearing off the balloon-covered paper from the large box, Meredith lifted the lid. Pushing back the tissue paper, she found a straw hat.

"It's to wear when we garden," Holly explained. "So you don't get too hot in the sun."

Meredith took it out of the box and tried it on.

Holly stood to one side and tilted her head. "It looks good."

While everyone seconded Holly, Meredith hugged the child she'd come to love. Daniel's daughter, Susie, toddled over to the coffee table and picked up the pretty pink bow that had decorated the package. Daniel scooped her up and set her on his knee.

"Open Dad's next," Holly ordered, bringing over a

small box wrapped in silver foil, topped with a white satin bow.

With her fingers trembling, Meredith detached the bow and tore off the paper. It was perfume. A very expensive brand with a floral scent she loved. She'd left a bottle of it on her vanity in her condo.

Turning to Cooper, she smiled at him, hoping he'd smile back. "Thank you."

He appeared to try to smile, but it didn't reach his eyes.

As Meredith opened the rest of the presents, she was acutely aware of him beside her. Although everyone else commented and joked, he remained silent and she wondered if he'd had an argument with Tina or received bad news of some sort. All of the presents and birthday wishes filled her heart, but then Cooper rose and went into the kitchen. She would have followed him except Holly insisted she open her perfume and spray some on.

A few minutes later Cooper returned to the room with a birthday cake, candles glowing. When he set it on the coffee table before her, he looked at her as if he didn't know her. While her guests sang "Happy Birthday," she made the wish that could fill her dreams and her life— she wished for a future with Cooper.

Alma insisted on helping Cooper cut the cake and serve the ice cream. When Meredith saw the assortment of food on the kitchen table for a buffet, she knew Cooper had put a lot of effort into this party. So what was making him so somber?

As everyone talked, ate and joked in the living room, Meredith escaped back out into the kitchen and found Cooper making a pot of coffee. "Thank you for a wonderful party."

"It's only balloons and a cake," he said evenly.

''And presents and people who've become my friends. I really appreciate it.''

''Look, Meredith. You don't have to pretend—''

Daniel came into the kitchen, Susie curled against his shoulder. ''Meredith, I just wanted to wish you happy birthday again before we leave. It's past Susie's bedtime.''

The toddler had poked her thumb into her mouth.

Meredith smiled at her and said to Daniel, ''Thank you for coming. And for the chocolates. They're one of my weaknesses.''

''Enjoy them. Cooper, I'll see you on the basketball court next Saturday.''

Cooper nodded and said, ''I'll walk you out.''

But as Daniel left the kitchen, and Cooper would have passed by her, Meredith clasped his arm. ''Cooper, what's wrong?''

Silence ticked between them like a bomb ready to go off. Finally he answered, ''When everyone leaves, Meredith, I'd like to see the present you received from your father.''

This time when she gazed into Cooper's eyes, she saw the doubts and suspicions and the pain of betrayal. Then he turned and followed Daniel to the front door.

Chapter Ten

The pink, white and blue balloons still bobbed at the ceiling in the living room as Meredith collected their guests' plates and plastic forks. Her heart seemed to beat in a staccato rhythm as she glanced up the stairs. She'd already said good-night to Holly and thanked her for her part in the party and the terrific straw hat. Cooper had stood silent by the bed as she'd hugged his daughter and left the room, afraid she might never be able to hug and say good-night to Holly again.

If he sent her away...

Her breath caught as she heard Cooper close Holly's door and start down the stairs. When he reached the bottom step, his gaze raked over her flowered skirt and blouse, over her, as if he was seeing her in a new light.

"Cooper..."

"Let's go into the kitchen," he said gruffly, and she knew he didn't want their voices to carry up to Holly's room.

When she reached the kitchen, Cooper stood at the

counter, his arms crossed over his chest. "Can I see the brooch?"

"How did you know...?"

"Your father called to wish you a happy birthday and mentioned it." Cooper's voice was matter of fact, unemotional, as if he were making conversation with a stranger.

She'd laid her purse on the foyer table after her guests had surprised her. Going to it now, she took out the butterfly pin and carried it to where Cooper stood. When she handed it to him, it looked so small and delicate against his large hand.

"That's quite a present. High-quality diamonds. Enough of them to light up the sky. Why didn't you wear it?"

"You *know* why I didn't wear it. Cooper, I was going to tell you tonight. After Holly went to bed."

His brows arched. "And I'm supposed to believe that lie along with the countless others you've told?"

Luke had said this could blow up in her face, and he'd been right. "I *never* lied to you. I wanted to teach. I became qualified to teach. My background was just an incidental I didn't think you had to know about."

The timbre of his voice was as foreboding as thunder. "Incidental? You consider it incidental that you don't *have* to work? That you're used to cooks and maids and diamonds?"

"I didn't mean to keep it from you. It just happened!"

"Deceit doesn't just happen, Meredith. What kind of fool do you think I am?"

Somehow she had to convince him to believe her...to convince him... "You weren't sure about me from the beginning. You were afraid to let someone else care for your daughter. I became attached to Holly...and you. I was afraid if I told you about my background, you'd send me away.''

"You're damn right about that!'' he exploded. "If I had known you were a debutante who wanted to dabble with a different life for amusement this summer, I never would have hired you. I can't believe Luke—''

"Don't blame Luke…or Becca. They knew I desperately wanted to teach.''

His gaze searched her. "I thought Becca came from a poor background. She spoke of going to live with her grandmother as a teenager, having Todd, working in her bakery before she met Luke. I never suspected—''

"It's complicated, Cooper. She turned her back on everything I grew up with to keep her son. It was partly because of Becca, as well as my divorce, that I knew I had to put some meaning in my life.''

"Meaning? By coming here and pretending to be someone you're not? What kind of meaning is that? Don't you understand the damage you've done here? Letting Holly get attached to you, knowing you'll be going back to your *real* life at the end of the summer?''

"Cooper, I didn't plan this. I didn't plan to fall in love with you—'' The hard resolve on his face stopped her.

"Love? You deceived me because you love me? How rich! I'm not sure there *is* such a thing as love between a man and a woman. There's need and there's passion, and when both are gone, any bond is broken. Love is only a figment of a woman's imagination—something that makes it easier for her to give her body to a man.''

She had deceived him, and he had every right to be angry. But he didn't have the right to belittle her feelings for him or arrogantly assume women deluded themselves about love!

"You're blind,'' she retorted. "And I know *lots* of men

who are just as blind.'' Holding the brooch in front of her, she gave it a shake. ''My father thinks presents can make up for the rushed phone calls and a work schedule that let us get a glimpse of him twice a week if we were lucky. Brian was blind to the necessity of spending time together as a couple to nurture our marriage, to talk about what mattered to us, to simply hold hands instead of having sex.''

Hardly even stopping for a breath, she pushed on. ''And you? You're blind to anything you don't want to see. Anything that makes you uncomfortable. Anything that makes you *feel*. You guard yourself so well, it practically takes a wrecking ball to get through. You're a strong, tender, arrogant man who wants to control his life *his* way. Sometimes that just isn't possible. Sometimes accidents happen, and sometimes people make mistakes. And sometimes you have to trust someone and believe in more than simply surviving from day to day. I *do* love you, Cooper, and it's no figment of my imagination!''

The silence in the kitchen practically rang in her ears. She thought she heard the creak of the stairs—

''I can't trust someone who didn't tell me the truth,'' he said factually with no emotion.

Suddenly Meredith realized Cooper's unshakable values would only let him see black and white. He couldn't accept her love, and her bank account wasn't even the issue. Her misrepresentation was. She'd deceived him. She was untrustworthy. And all her declarations of love wouldn't matter. A bleakness settled over her heart that she knew would shadow her for a very long time.

''Do you want me to leave tonight or can I say goodbye to Holly in the morning?''

The nerve in his jaw worked as he silently debated her

question. Finally he answered, "You can leave in the morning."

Attempting to contain her love, just trying to keep the tears at bay and hold herself together until she reached her room, she nodded. If Cooper would give her merely an inkling that they had a chance...

But his eyes were cold, his expression hard, and she knew they didn't. Leaving the kitchen, she ran up the stairs to her room. When she closed the door, her tears fell, and she knew she'd lost the love of her life.

Sliding the few pieces of leftover birthday cake onto a dish, Cooper stared at it, then with an oath dumped it into the trash can. He wouldn't want any reminder of Meredith or the party once she'd left.

Once she'd left.

With more force than he intended, he tossed a soda can into the plastic bin. It hit the side and bounced out again.

"Why are you sending Meredith away like you did Mommy?"

Holly's voice startled him; he hadn't heard her bare feet on the wood floor. Her words made him suck in a breath as he realized she blamed him for Tina leaving. Moving the trash can out of his path, he crossed to his daughter. "I didn't send your mom away."

Holly's little hands were tight balls by her side. "Yes, you did. I heard you. You thought I was sleeping. But I wanted to know why Mommy was crying. I was sitting at the top of the steps. You told her to leave!"

The past two years had dulled the memory of his final argument with Tina but hadn't erased it. He'd been working in his shop and when he'd come inside, Tina had said they had to talk. She'd explained in detail what she wanted for her life, and it didn't include him. When she'd asked him for a divorce, yes, she had been crying. But she'd also been certain their marriage was over. In pain, he'd told her to leave that night. She'd come back the next morning to talk to Holly and pack her things.

"I told your mom to leave because that was what she wanted. She'd already made up her mind, Holly. She wanted to move to New York."

His daughter's eyes glistened. "Why couldn't we go with her?"

Suddenly he realized his daughter thought he hadn't tried to save their marriage. And maybe he hadn't because he'd known it was hopeless. He couldn't have lived in New York City any more than Tina could have stayed in Harmony Hollow. Pulling out a chair, he sat and opened his arms to Holly.

When she came to him, he put his arms around her. "You know how when we first found the kittens, they were happy to stay in the box?"

With a nod, Holly murmured, "They didn't try to get out."

"That's right. And then they did start getting out and we kept them in your room with the door closed."

"So they wouldn't get lost."

"Uh-huh. But now they want to run all over the house."

"And outside," Holly added.

He gave her a little squeeze. "And outside. They want to explore the world. And they'll never stay in that box again. Your mommy is sort of like Daisy and Muffin. For a while she was happy here with us, in this house, in Harmony Hollow. But then she wanted more. More excitement. More opportunities. More people to meet."

"And she'll never be happy here again?"

"She feels trapped here, small stuff. She needs more

room than I and Harmony Hollow can give her. And she wants to show you that great big world outside of Harmony Hollow.''

''In New York.''

''And other places she'll probably want to take you when you're older.''

Holly looked down at the hem of her nightie. ''So why are you sending Meredith away when she likes our box?''

If Cooper's thoughts weren't in such an uproar, he might have smiled. But he couldn't smile after what had happened. Taking Holly's chin in his hand, he tilted her face up. ''Were you sitting on the stairs listening?''

''I went for a drink in the bathroom and I heard your voice get loud.''

''Meredith didn't tell me something very important about herself.''

''Why?''

''Because she thought I wouldn't like it.''

''She was afraid,'' Holly determined as if she could imagine exactly how Meredith felt. And it hit him with force that she probably could. It had only been since Meredith's arrival and with her support that Holly had become more open with him about so many things.

Meredith had called him arrogant. Was he so arrogant that the people he cared about couldn't talk to him or trust him to understand? What if he had listened better to Tina when they were married? After she sold her book, maybe he had been as blind as Meredith had said, and that's why Tina's decision to divorce him had been such a devastating blow.

''I don't want Meredith to go away. I want her to be my substitute mom.'' Holly's chin quivered, and her unhappiness squeezed his heart.

''Holly, she just came for the summer.''

"I *know* she wants to stay. I heard her say she loves you. And she *likes* going rock hunting and playing in the garden, *and* swinging on the swing. She likes Daisy and Muffin and Gypsy. Are you going to make her go away jus' because she was afraid to tell you something?"

In other words, *was* he an unforgiving fool? Didn't he want Meredith to stay *more* than his daughter did? Didn't he want to believe in a happy future, much more than surviving from day to day? Didn't he want to believe in love?

Anger at Tina had clouded his life for so long. When he'd begun to feel other emotions, they'd made him uncomfortable. Finding out Meredith had kept something from him had given him an excuse to latch on to the anger again—because it was familiar.

Did he want familiar?

Or did he want Meredith, with her caring and beauty and intelligence as well as her background? But would *she* forgive *him?* His tunnel vision and righteous arrogance?

He didn't know. But he wouldn't find out sitting here. Standing, he ruffled Holly's hair. "You know, you're pretty wise for your age. But Meredith might be very angry at me right now and *want* to leave." His gut tightened when he thought about what he'd said to her, how he'd denied what he'd felt for her all these weeks, how he'd rejected her love. If she really meant what she'd said, if she could be happy here... "I'm going to talk to her and ask her to stay. But you have to promise me you'll stay in bed and keep your door shut."

"You'll come and tell me what she says?"

He guided his daughter to the stairway. "I'll tell you what she says."

As he tucked Holly in again and patted Muffin's nose, his heart raced. He was trying to be casual with his daughter, yet felt anything *but* casual. Standing at Meredith's closed door, he knocked twice.

She opened the door, and he saw that she'd changed into her nightgown and robe. Her eyes were puffy as if she'd been crying, and his chest tightened around his racing heart. On the bed her suitcase lay open, half-filled.

"Can I come in?" When she hesitated, he added, "I don't want Holly to overhear."

Meredith's hands went to the belt of her robe, and she tightened it as she backed up. When he closed the door, she moved away and stood by the chair at the window.

"Why didn't you tell me about your background?"

"I told you, it didn't matter."

"The truth, Meredith."

Her cheeks flushed. "You didn't like Tina's new lifestyle which was somewhat like my old one. I knew you'd jump to conclusions and think we were alike."

And he probably would have. Meredith knew him so well, it was embarrassing. "Harmony Hollow wasn't enough for Tina. *I* wasn't enough for Tina."

Shaking her head, Meredith said, "Tina's dreams are different from mine, Cooper. I've *seen* what money can buy. And what it can't buy is even more important. It can't buy a good marriage or affection or even self-esteem. I needed meaning in my life. I forgot about who I used to be and the balance in my bank account to become a teacher. When I came here, I found even more meaning in taking care of Holly…and you. I never expected to fall in love. I didn't particularly *want* to fall in love."

"Neither did I," he said in a low voice.

Her eyes widened, and she looked stunned.

He still felt that way himself. Approaching her slowly, he cleared his throat. "I told Holly I'd ask you to stay. But I want more than a teacher for my daughter and a housekeeper for me. I want *you.* In every way there is—in my life, in my bed, in my thoughts.''

"But you said you couldn't trust me. You said—''

He couldn't keep from wanting her, from loving her, from touching her. Reaching out, he stroked her cheek. "I'm sorry for what I said. For how I acted. Can you forgive me for being so blind, for making what I felt into so much less than it was?''

Covering his hand with hers, she held his gaze and said, "Of course, I can forgive you. I love you.''

Then he took her into his arms and gathered her close. "Will you marry me?'' he murmured.

Her radiant smile answered him before she did. "Yes, I'll marry you.'' Suddenly the smile vanished. "But if you want more children, I don't know if I can carry one—''

"I want *you,* Meredith. And if we're blessed with children, we'll thank God. If not, we'll love Holly and each other for the rest of our lives.'' His lips sealed to hers, promising her a future and a lifetime of love.

Breaking from the kiss, he leaned his forehead against hers. "There is one problem.''

"What?'' she asked, worry trembling in the word.

"Your money. Or whatever you have. I have to feel as if I'm providing for us.''

"I want to be a partner in our marriage, Cooper.''

One of the things he loved most about Meredith was her ability to stand her ground with him. "You'll be a partner, whether you decide to stay at home or teach or start an interior decorating service. But what you already have...''

"Do you want me to give my money to charity?'' she asked seriously.

He could see Meredith would do that for him...for them, and he realized Tina's sudden income had had little bearing on the breakup of their marriage and his bitterness toward her. It was the difference in their goals and dreams that had torn them apart, Tina's inability to keep a promise he'd considered sacred. Meredith shared his goals and dreams, just as she understood the sacredness of marriage vows.

And if he wanted a marriage that could weather all storms, he knew he had to compromise. "You can do whatever you want with your money," he answered, then added teasingly, "Maybe we *should* save some for our retirement."

She laughed, wrapped her arms tighter around his neck and kissed him again.

That kiss led to another and another until Cooper took her down on the bed with him. A short time later, he groaned and pushed himself away from her, his breathing ragged. "I promised Holly I'd tell her if you're staying."

Her hair mussed, her cheeks flushed, her lips kissed pink, Meredith murmured, "Then you should keep your promise."

He took her hand and kissed her palm. "We'll tell her together. How soon should we get married?"

"How soon do you *want* to get married?" she joked.

"Tomorrow," he said with a straight face. "But if you want a big wedding—"

"I don't need a big wedding. As soon as we can arrange it will suit me just fine."

"I am *really* glad you said that. Because...I'd like to wait to make love. Until we *are* married. Because of Holly...and because of the way you feel about making love. I want to start our marriage the *right* way." When her lips curved up, he asked, "Am I being arrogant again?"

With loving tenderness she stroked his jaw and responded, "A little. But I don't mind because I feel the same way."

Smiling, he brought her close to him for another kiss—
a kiss that promised again he'd love her for the rest of
their lives.

With the help of family and friends, Meredith and Cooper had planned their wedding in two weeks. It was amaz-
ing, really, Meredith thought as she sat before a mirror in
the small dressing room at the back of the church, letting
Becca attach her veil.

"You look like a princess," Holly said with awe as she
gazed up at Meredith.

In the mirror, Meredith saw her reflection with the pearl
tiara, delicate veil and ivory gown with its princess-lined
bodice accented with re-embroidered lace and seed pearls.
She looked radiant—a happy woman...a woman in love.

Turning, she smiled down at Holly. "You do, too. And
so do Becca and Paula."

Holly was wearing the same style sea-green taffeta and
chiffon gown as Meredith's attendants.

Paula, her auburn hair adorned with a headpiece of tiny
white lilies and green tulle, clasped Meredith's arm. "It's
time."

Meredith took a deep breath, gathered her full skirt and
stood facing the little girl and two women who were so
important in her life. "Let's go to a wedding."

After hugs and tears, Becca opened the door, and Meredith stepped into the vestibule where her father was waiting.

"You're sure about this?" Phillip Preston asked som-
berly.

"Never more sure of anything. Be happy for me, Dad."

Finally, he smiled. "I am. And I wish you all the happiness you deserve."

As flower girl, Holly proceeded down the aisle first,
scattering rose petals as she stepped in practiced pace to

the soft organ music. Paula followed her and then Becca. When the organist began the classical processional, everyone in the church looked toward the doors and waited. Meredith squeezed her dad's arm and they began walking. She smiled, glanced at the people gathered, both new friends and old, her stepmother and Gran, Todd and Luke. Then her gaze quickly passed over Daniel and Jake and finally rested on Cooper. He'd never looked more handsome than he did at that moment in his black tux and white shirt with black tie.

But as she approached him, it was the expression in his eyes that took her breath away. There was such a world of love there, just waiting for her to claim it. When her father gave her hand to Cooper, he thanked the older man, then escorted her to their position before the Reverend. Meredith was hardly aware of the words of the service, though they were a background for everything she wanted to give Cooper and everything he wanted to give her.

When it came time to exchange vows, her voice trembled with the importance and the sacredness of what she was doing. Cooper's words were strong, steady and true. She felt tears fill her eyes as he promised to cherish her always. Because she knew he would. As they exchanged rings, they gazed into each others' eyes, giving their hearts, too. After the final blessing, Cooper took her into his arms and kissed her long and sweetly until everyone began applauding. Then he raised his head, grinned at her and escorted her down the aisle to the back of the church where he kissed her all over again.

"Finally," he murmured in her ear as guests started coming toward them. "Finally you're mine."

They held their reception in the church's social hall. Paula had insisted on taking care of decorating it for them. White cloths covered the tables, and there were candelabras and flower arrangements everywhere. It was beautifully done, and Meredith thanked her sister repeatedly, just as she'd thanked Daniel and Jake for the rehearsal dinner they'd thrown the night before at a restaurant in Manchester. Everything about the day passed so swiftly that Meredith was glad they'd have it all on videotape, as well as in photographs.

After a buffet dinner, the three-piece band—also Paula's doing—began playing. Cutting the cake was a sensual experience, as Cooper fed her, brushed icing from her lip and then kissed the sweetness away. She fed him, letting her fingers linger on his jaw and watched the passion that she knew they'd share that night blaze in his eyes.

Cooper couldn't seem to take his gaze from her, and finally he said, "I've never seen you look more beautiful."

"Not even when Spark dumped me?" she teased.

He laughed. "That runs a close second." Then his expression became serious as he held his hand out to her. "May I have the first dance of our married life?"

"You may have all my dances," she responded.

At a nod from Cooper, the band began to play the waltz that they'd danced to on the dock the night of the Strawberry Festival. Tears came to her eyes again. "You remembered."

"I remember everything about you...about us. That night when we danced...I think I began to realize what you could mean to my life." Leading her to the dance floor, he took her into his arms and waltzed her into their future.

Epilogue

Eleven months later
A Sunday afternoon

When Cooper's lips touched her forehead, Meredith came awake.

"Hey, pretty mama, Nancy's downstairs. She brought something for the baby."

Meredith's hand automatically went to her very round tummy. She was due in two weeks. Her pregnancy had been a surprise, but a welcome one. Even Holly was excited and couldn't wait to have a baby brother or sister.

The first trimester had been scary. But Cooper had listened to her worries, soothed her fears and prayed with her every night that their child would go full term. Their prayers had been answered.

Levering herself up, her back aching more than in the morning, Meredith said, "If the little one would stop kicking at night, I wouldn't need these afternoon naps."

Cooper tenderly stroked her abdomen. "I seem to remember some very enjoyable afternoon naps."

His lazy smile thrilled her as it always did. It told her he still desired her. After Holly returned to school in the fall, Cooper would sometimes surprise Meredith by coming home for lunch and continuing to nurture the passion that had overwhelmed them both on their wedding night. Everyday, in a hundred ways, he showed her how happy he was she'd become his wife. She'd learned early on he was a man of action rather than words, but in the dark of night when they held each other close, the words came, too. She'd never thought she could *be* this happy.

He kissed her softly, slowly, with a lingering desire that told her he wished they didn't have company waiting downstairs.

After he ended the kiss, she slid her legs over the side of the bed. "I probably look a sight."

His gaze swept over her pink-knit maternity top and slacks. "You look beautiful."

Laughing, she shook her head. "You're biased."

After quickly running a brush through her hair, she slipped on leather sandals and joined him in the doorway. He let her precede him down the hall and the steps.

Halfway down she heard a whisper, then a low giggle, and as she reached the bottom at least ten people called, "Surprise!"

Nancy was in the living room, all right, along with Meredith's sister Paula and their stepmother, Becca and her grandmother, Luke and Todd, Alma, Clarice and a few teachers Meredith had come to know at Holly's school. Then there was Holly, pointing to a beautiful pine cradle sitting in the middle of the room. "Dad made it for you," she said with pride.

Meredith turned to the man who was strength and love

and everything she'd ever imagined in a husband. Throwing her arms around his neck, tears fell down her cheeks. "Oh, Cooper."

He kissed her cheek, then, resting his chin on the crown of her head, he told the friends and relatives, "It's hormones. She does this a lot."

Leaning back, she playfully swatted his shoulder. As she turned once again toward the guests, she remembered her birthday party last July and what had followed. She glanced at Cooper. His brown eyes told her he remembered, too.

"We've come a long way," he murmured, taking her hand and then guiding her into the room to a place of honor in the rocker. All at once everyone started talking.

As she opened presents ranging from disposable diapers, rattles and terry playsuits to a beautiful sweater set crocheted by Becca's grandmother, Meredith discovered all of her out-of-town guests were staying overnight at an inn in Harmony Hollow. She was glad she'd have some time to spend with them.

With only two presents left, Meredith unwrapped one from Tina. Opening the box, she found a baby book. Inside the front cover Tina had written: "For all the precious moments you'll treasure always."

Meredith handed it to Cooper. He and his ex-wife had a workable relationship now—one in which they put Holly's interests first. They still disagreed now and then, but the animosity was gone and they compromised for Holly's sake.

Knowing Holly was waiting for her to open the last present—hers—Meredith tore the paper from a stuffed pony the nine-year-old had chosen for her new brother or sister. When Meredith hugged the child she'd come to love as her own, a sharp pain stabbed her back and she inhaled quickly. But the pain dulled and she decided the baby must have changed position.

A short time later as everyone served themselves from the buffet Becca had helped Cooper set up in the kitchen, another sudden stab made Meredith hurry to the living room where she sat and took a deep breath.

Apparently Cooper had been watching because in an instant he was by her side asking, "What's wrong?"

Before she could answer, another sensation made her gasp. "I think my water just broke."

Cooper shouted for Becca, and the next half hour passed in a fast-forward blur. Meredith found herself in her husband's arms as he carried her to Luke's van. Luke drove, while Cooper sat with her in the back holding her hand, reassuring Holly who was in the seat behind them that everything was fine, just a little ahead of schedule.

At the hospital a nurse whisked Meredith away to a birthing room that she and Cooper and Holly had toured a month before. It seemed only minutes later that Cooper, dressed in blue scrubs, stood beside her, offering her ice chips and reminding her how to breathe through contractions.

"Where's Holly?" Meredith asked during a calmer moment.

Tenderly Cooper brushed his wife's hair from her forehead. "She's in the lounge with Becca, Paula and Luke. Todd stayed with Gran and your stepmother at the house. I called Daniel and Jake. They said they're coming over. I told them they didn't have to, but they seem to think I need moral support." He said the last with a teasing grin.

Both Daniel and Jake were in and out of their house often. Daniel had been much easier to get to know than Jake, who guarded himself as well as Cooper used to. But she liked them both and considered them friends of hers now, too.

Suddenly a contraction hit that was much more intense than all the rest. As she squeezed Cooper's hand and breathed, fear washed over her. But her husband seemed to sense it. Putting his arm around her, supporting her, he murmured in her ear, "I love you. Everything's going to be fine."

Her panic seemed to fade with the contraction and when the next one came, she was ready.

Her obstetrician replaced the nurse at the foot of the birthing chair and began coaching on when to push. It seemed to be a century later when he said, "I see the head. There it is, Meredith. Give it all you've got."

Cooper held her as she pushed with all her might and seconds later heard, "It's a boy!" and the first cry of their son.

Meredith was crying, too, as the nurse placed the baby at her breast. A tear slid down Cooper's cheek as he took his son's little hand between his fingers and whispered, "Thank you, Meredith."

When she wiped the tear from her husband's strong jaw, she smiled at him and murmured back, "Thank you, Cooper. Does the name we picked out fit?"

"Shane Thomas Murphy. It couldn't fit any better."

Then her husband lowered his head and, right before he kissed her, she whispered, "I love you, Cooper Murphy. For now and for always."

His lips found hers and renewed the vows they'd made on their wedding day—to love, honor and cherish for a lifetime.

*   *   *   *   *

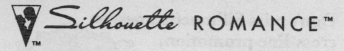

Silhouette ROMANCE™

Join *Silhouette Romance*
as more couples experience
the joy only babies
can bring!

Bundles
of JOY

September 1999
THE BABY BOND
by Lilian Darcy (SR #1390)

Tom Callahan a daddy? Impossible! Yet that was before Julie Gregory showed up
with the shocking news that she carried his child. Now the father-to-be knew
marriage was the answer!

October 1999
BABY, YOU'RE MINE
by Lindsay Longford (SR #1396)

Marriage was the *last* thing on Murphy Jones's mind when he invited
beautiful—and pregnant—Phoebe McAllister to stay with him. But then
she and her newborn bundle filled his house with laughter...and had bachelor
Murphy rethinking his no-strings lifestyle....

And in December 1999, popular author

MARIE FERRARELLA

brings you

THE BABY BENEATH THE MISTLETOE (SR #1408)

Available at your favorite retail outlet.

Silhouette®

Silhouette

ROMANCE™

COMING NEXT MONTH

#1408 THE BABY BENEATH THE MISTLETOE—Marie Ferrarella
Bundles of Joy
Natural-born nurturer Michelle Rozanski wasn't about to let Tony Marino face instant fatherhood alone. Even if Tony could be gruffer than a hibernating bear, he'd made a place in his home—and heart—for an abandoned child. And now if Michelle had her way, they'd *never* face parenthood alone!

#1409 EXPECTING AT CHRISTMAS—Charlotte Maclay
When his butler was away, the *last* replacement millionaire Griffin Jones expected was eight-months-pregnant Loretta Santana. Yet somehow she'd charmed him into hiring her. And now this confirmed bachelor found himself falling for Loretta...and her Christmas-baby-on-the-way....

#1410 EMMA AND THE EARL—Elizabeth Harbison
Cinderella Brides
She thought she'd outgrown dreams of happily-ever-after, yet when American Emma Lawrence found herself a guest of Earl Brice Palliser's lavish estate, he seemed her very own Prince Charming come to life. But was there a place in Brice's noble heart for plain Emma?

#1411 A DIAMOND FOR KATE—Moyra Tarling
The moment devastatingly handsome Dr. Marshall Diamond entered the hospital, nurse Kate Turner recognized him as the man she'd secretly loved as a child. But could Kate convince him that the girl from his past was now a woman he could trust...forever?

#1412 THE MAN, THE RING, THE WEDDING—Patricia Thayer
With These Rings
Tall, dark and *rich* John Rossi was cozying up to innocent Angelina Covelli for one reason—revenge. But old family feuds weren't sweet enough to keep the sexy CEO fixed on his goal. His mind—and heart—kept steering him to Angelina...and rings...and weddings!

#1413 THE MILLIONAIRE'S PROPOSITION—Natalie Patrick
Waitress Becky Taylor was tempted to accept Clark Winstead's proposal. It was an enticing offer—a handsome millionaire, a rich life, family. If only it wasn't lacking a few elements...like a wedding...and love. Good thing Becky was planning to do a little enticing of her own....